Metal crunched against metal.

Their pursuers slammed into the vehicle's back end.

Shae braced her hands against the dashboard. "You have to slow for the bridge. It's about a mile from here."

"Is there any other way around?" Mason asked.

"No."

Mason rounded a curve, and the bridge loomed ahead of them. The wood railings had long ago begun to rot, probably along with most of the other boards. The joints creaked and moaned as he hit the bridge—then slammed on his brakes when another vehicle blocked the far end of their path.

They were trapped.

The other driver accelerated. Mason tried to maneuver around him on the narrow structure, but their attacker's car hit them from the side.

Mason's head cracked hard against the driver's side window as he and Shae spun. Darkness encroached in his peripheral vision. The car hit the railing. With one loud groan, the rail gave way and they were airborne, plunging toward the black swamp water below...

Deena Alexander grew up in a small town on eastern Long Island where she lived up until a few years ago and then relocated to Clermont, Florida, with her husband, three children, son-in-law and four dogs. Now she enjoys long walks in nature all year long, despite the occasional alligator or snake she sometimes encounters. Her love for writing developed after the birth of her youngest son, who had trouble sleeping through the night.

Books by Deena Alexander

Love Inspired Suspense

Crime Scene Connection
Shielding the Tiny Target
Kidnapped in the Woods
Christmas in the Crosshairs
Hunted for the Holidays

Visit the Author Profile page at LoveInspired.com.

Hunted for the Holidays

DEENA ALEXANDER

LOVE INSPIRED SUSPENSE
INSPIRATIONAL ROMANCE

LOVE INSPIRED® SUSPENSE
INSPIRATIONAL ROMANCE

Recycling programs
for this product may
not exist in your area.

ISBN-13: 978-1-335-98023-6

Hunted for the Holidays

Copyright © 2024 by Denise Pysarchuk

Love Inspired
22 Adelaide St. West, 41st Floor
Toronto, Ontario M5H 4E3, Canada
www.LoveInspired.com

Printed in Lithuania

MIX
Paper | Supporting
responsible forestry
FSC® C021394

Seek the Lord, and his strength:
seek his face evermore.
—*Psalms* 105:4

To my agent, Dawn Dowdle, you were the first to believe in me, and I will be forever grateful.

ONE

Cheers erupted as Gracie Evans, Shae's five-year-old daughter, smiled at the audience, waved and did a little impromptu dance that had nothing to do with her role as a sheep in the church's annual Christmas pageant. Her long, dark ponytail swung, and the stage lights made her sapphire eyes sparkle. Some of the older actors glanced at the director, then continued with their lines as Gracie jumped and wiggled, her mischievous grin charming the cheering crowd. Shae applauded loudly with the rest of the families. "Go, Gracie!"

Seconds later, an angel corralled the little girl and guided her to her proper position, and Shae checked her phone camera to be sure it was still recording. As she looked back up, satisfied she hadn't missed any of the theatrics, her gaze landed on two men dressed in dark suits standing to the side of the auditorium, their expressions harsh as they scanned the spectators rather than watching the action on stage.

No! For just an instant, recognition flared, followed almost immediately by uncertainty. Even if one of them did look familiar, who was to say it was someone from her past? Perhaps she'd met one of these men after relocating to Boggy Meadows. Still…fear flooded her system.

Because if it was someone from before… How could they have found her? They couldn't have. It wasn't possible. At least, that was what the marshals had assured her when they'd placed her in the witness protection program six years ago. Besides, Quentin Kincaid was in prison and would be for the rest of his life, thanks in large part to Shae's testimony. Could he have escaped?

In some part of her mind, she equated the applause and jubilation surrounding her with Gracie and knew her daughter must be drawing attention again, but Shae had missed it, distracted by what could be a death sentence for them both. She refocused the camera on the stage, needing to capture what might be their last moment of normalcy before the past caught up with her. No use. She held her phone up to block her face but marked the men's progress up the side aisle.

She plastered on a smile, but her cheers caught in her throat, nearly choking her. Her mouth went dry, then her shouts turned internal. She had to get her daughter off that stage and out of there.

Sweat beaded Shae's brow. She swiped at it with the back of her wrist and glanced at the clock. Run and risk drawing attention? Or stay put until the show ended and mix with the crowd to make her escape?

Maybe the two men had just arrived late and were searching for family members, but then why were the little hairs on the back of her neck standing straight up? The goose bumps racing across her skin had nothing to do with the air-conditioning, of that she had no doubt. As she waited for the pageant to end and the actors to take their bows, Shae planned escape routes and calculated the distance to exits until the curtain was finally dragged closed.

Keeping her head down and face averted behind the bouquet she'd brought Gracie, she slung her oversize bag onto her shoulder, slid into the stream of spectators and started toward the cafeteria, where other parents had already begun to gather.

"Mommy!" Gracie ran toward her, cheeks flushed, grinning from ear to ear. "Did you see? I did a dance on the stage. It was a surprise."

"It was awesome, honey. I loved it. You were amazing." Shae reminded herself not to use Gracie's name in case the men knew it. She forced an answering smile and hugged her daughter close, then handed her the flowers, shielding her as best she could.

"Thank you. They're so pretty." Gracie stuck her nose in the bouquet and inhaled deeply.

"Just like you, sweetie." As Shae kissed her daughter's head, her gaze skipped to the exits. Only one parent per child was allowed to pick the actors up from the cafeteria, which gave her a brief reprieve. But which way should she go? "Do you have your bag?"

"Uh-huh." Gracie lifted the sparkly silver duffel bag she'd fallen in love with when she'd spotted it at the holiday fair. "Got it."

Shae pulled the white sheep costume over Gracie's head, leaving her in black leggings and a long-sleeved black T-shirt, then stuffed the costume they'd worked together on all week into the bag. "All right. Let's go."

She hugged Gracie against her leg, keeping an arm wrapped firmly around her so she could hold her close and not chance losing track of her. She watched for trouble as they inched through the doorway. With so many people milling about, actors stopping in the lobby to meet up with the rest of their families and take pictures, and a small crowd already headed toward the parking lot in anticipation of getting out ahead of the rush, Shae had lost sight of the men. But the niggle at the base of her neck told her they were still lurking, still searching.

She might not be so on edge if her handler, the woman who'd placed her in the small town of Boggy Meadows, Florida, hadn't recently been killed in a car crash nearby. According to the news reports, it had been a tragic accident, but Shae wasn't buying that. Maria Delarosa had had no business in Boggy Meadows unless she'd been trying to reach Shae. To warn her? She had no idea. All she knew was that she had to protect Gracie at all costs, which meant she needed to be somewhere else, anywhere else, as soon as possible. No matter what was going on, their time in Boggy Meadows had come to an end.

"Awesome job, Gracie! Ice cream's on me." Reva MacMillan, the director and mom of Gracie's best friend, Katie, patted Gracie's back and gestured toward a group of kids. "We're all meeting up at Jimmie's."

"Yay!" Gracie high-fived Katie. "Can we get ice cream, Mommy?"

Shae could only offer a noncommittal grunt. She had no intention of telling anyone she wasn't going to Jimmie's with the cast. If her pursuers caught wind of the planned get-together and detoured to the ice cream parlor in search of her, it might give her a couple of extra minutes to gather a few necessities and run. She was already compiling in her head a list of things she had to pack and kicking herself for not keeping their flight bags up-to-date. Gracie had probably grown two sizes since she'd last filled the bags with clothes. Oh, well, they could buy what they needed once they got away.

"Mommy!" Gracie yanked her hand, staring at her with a frustrated exasperation that told Shae she'd already called her more than once.

"Huh? What, sweetie?" Shae scanned the parking lot as they finally stepped out into the muggy Florida night.

"I said, can Katie come in our car to get ice cream?"

With both girls staring hopefully, and no good excuse to say no, Shae faltered.

"Mo-ommy." Gracie frowned. "Did you hear me?"

"Uh, yeah. I'm sorry, I'm a little distracted." Shae braced herself for the pout. "Katie can't ride with us tonight, hon. I'm sorry, but I need to make a stop. We'll see you later, okay, Katie?"

Katie sent Shae a confused scowl before taking Reva's hand.

The two girls had become close, despite Shae's reluctance, and often spent afternoons at the park together and weekends playing soccer and attending faith formation. If it had been up to Shae, Gracie would have remained home all the time, where she could keep an eye on her, keep her safe. But Gracie, ever the social butterfly, had other ideas, and Shae did want her to have a normal life.

With that, she urged Gracie toward the car.

"We'll see you at Jimmie's, Katie!" Shae called out loud enough to be overheard if anyone cared to listen.

A dark sedan turned into the lot, battling its way upstream against the outgoing tide of cars.

Her heart thundered. She had to get out of there without being seen or any chance of escape would be gone.

And not only would these men kill her and her daughter, they wouldn't hesitate to take out the whole crowd of innocent bystanders in pursuit of that goal.

Gracie lifted a hand and opened her mouth to call out to a friend.

Shae pulled her closer. "Be quiet, Gracie, and go to the car."

Gracie's eyes went wide—Shae never snapped at her—and then she whined, "But, Mom—"

"Shh. Remember cheesemonkey?" As much as she hated to use the secret code word they'd decided upon in case of an emergency, and had hoped to get Gracie out of there without scaring her or making her react in a way that might draw attention, Shae needed her to stop asking questions and move.

Gracie's steps faltered as she frowned up at Shae. "For real or for practice?"

Tell her the truth or let her maintain a blessed sense of innocence for just a little while longer? Vigilance was more important—which she couldn't maintain if Gracie didn't cooperate. She leaned close and whispered, "Real, honey. Just do like we practiced and everything will be fine."

Gracie pressed closer against Shae's leg. "Are we still gonna go for ice cream?"

Shae searched for which parking lot exit was least used. If she got caught up in the mess of strolling families and slow-moving vehicles, she'd be an easy target. "Don't say another word. Just get to the car. Now."

The dirty look the little girl shot her could have knocked her on her duff, but at least Gracie sulked quietly as she trod beside Shae, her glittery bag thumping against her leg in a steady rhythm that matched the pounding in Shae's skull. And at least she had her head down, making it more difficult to identify her if the men stalking them had pictures. Would they recognize Gracie? Did they even know about her? Probably. But why risk coming after them at a children's Christmas pageant? Why not grab them at home, where they would be less likely to be interrupted? If they'd managed to find her at the church she attended, surely they knew her address.

Unless their house was already under surveillance by the FBI or the marshals' service, and the men pursuing her somehow knew it. Had that been what Maria was doing there? Had they left Shae and Gracie in place as bait? Anger welled.

She massaged her temples as a ruse to cover her face and look around. No. She refused to believe Maria would have agreed to that, would have had any part of it without warning Shae. But… Maria was dead. And she had been near Boggy Meadows when she was killed. What if someone with less of a moral compass was calling the shots?

Shae hit the button on her key fob to unlock the doors, then looked around and opened the back door for Gracie. Once her daughter was safely inside, Shae climbed into the driver's seat, stuck the key in the ignition and hesitated. What if they'd rigged the car with explosives? Maybe it would be safer to flee on foot.

No. She had to stop second-guessing herself. Surely if they'd already rigged the car, they wouldn't be hanging around the parking lot waiting to get blown up.

She held her breath—*God, please don't let the car explode*—and turned the key. No bomb. Well, that was a relief. But that was when she spotted the two men again, weaving between cars, peeking in windows. "Get on the floor, Gracie."

"Wh-what about my b-booster seat?" The one she'd felt so grown-up moving into.

"Don't worry about it." A quick glance in her rearview mirror showed Gracie's shocked expression. "Cheese-monkey, remember? Get on the floor, pull the blanket from the back seat over you and hide. Do it, Gracie. Now."

Either the code word or her tone must have gotten through to her daughter that this was no joke, because she slid onto the floor, still clutching her flowers, and pulled the blanket they'd used at the drive-in movie what seemed like a lifetime ago over her head. Shae inched forward into the line of cars exiting the lot.

"M-Mommy?" The shakiness in Gracie's usually confident voice beat at Shae. "I'm scared."

"I know, honey, and I'm sorry. I'll explain everything. I promise." *As soon as I lose these goons and we get on the road.*

"Are the storms coming now?"

"What st…?" Oh, right. She'd forgotten Gracie had heard the weather report this morning—possibly severe storms—which had terrified her. But that was the least of Shae's problems. Florida often had storms, though the meteorologist had said these could bring tornadoes as well, thanks to El Niño. She wouldn't have given it a second thought if not for Gracie's fear of thunder. But she didn't have time for that right now. God willing, they'd be long gone from Florida in a few hours and wouldn't have to worry about any storms. The men trolling the parking lot were a much more immediate concern. "No, baby. No storms."

"O-okay." Gracie cried softly beneath the blanket on what was supposed to be such a special night, a night that should have been so filled with joy.

The phone number Shae had committed to memory six years before and had prayed she'd never need ran through her head over and over again, like a mantra. Should she call now? No. She had to stay focused on escape first. The call could be made from home. Even if someone were nearby to help, they'd never make it to her before she got out of the parking lot. Besides, she wasn't even a hundred percent sure she'd use the number. She was supposed to contact the marshals' service any time she planned to move, but what good had witness protection done her if Kincaid's men had found her? What if this was a repeat of the first time a leak somewhere in the FBI had led Kincaid straight to her?

When she finally made her way out of the lot, she resisted the urge to slam her foot down on the gas pedal—barely—but she didn't breathe a sigh of relief until they'd rounded two corners and she'd checked her rearview mirror more than a dozen times.

At a stop sign, she twisted around and said, "You can get up now, Gracie."

The little girl peered from beneath the blanket, glanced around and sniffed.

"I'm sorry, sweetheart." Where should she start? She should have had plenty of time to talk to Gracie about her past. She'd eventually have to tell her in order to keep her safe and make sure she stayed alert when she went out alone, but she should have had years before that became a concern. How did you explain to a five-year-old that bad men were trying to kill them?

Gracie crawled into her booster seat and sulked.

And Shae took the coward's way out and said nothing. Instead, myriad questions ricocheted around her head. Was she being paranoid? Or had someone actually found her? Certainly, there could be another reason two men in suits were scanning the crowd at a children's pageant, then peering in car windows throughout the parking lot. Just because one of them might have looked familiar didn't necessarily mean they were dangerous. Even if Maria Delarosa *had* been killed. But she couldn't come up with any other explanation, except…

She'd been found, which should have been impossible. But Kincaid's men had done it before, during the trial. She'd been forced to flee the safe house they'd arranged for her when one of the FBI agents charged with protecting her had betrayed them, another had been killed and another, the one who mattered to her more than anyone else, had gone missing.

Gone rogue? Gotten killed? Turned dirty? No one she'd spoken to knew.

But he'd disappeared after a yearlong relationship and one night of passion—a night Shae couldn't bring herself to regret, despite the outcome, because it had given her Gracie, her reason for living. Clearly God had forgiven her that moment of weakness since He'd blessed her with such an amazing daughter. Now, if only He'd protect her.

Shae took the turn into her driveway too fast, hit the button to open the garage door, waited impatiently as the door lumbered open and shot inside the instant it cleared her roof level. She debated leaving the door open so she could escape quickly, then decided to close it. Better if no one saw her packing up the car. She could always back through the garage door if necessary.

"Go straight in the house, dump your bag out on the floor and stuff whatever is most important to you inside, just like we practiced, okay?" Shae swung the car door open then turned to stare at her trembling daughter. "Gracie, listen to me. Everything will be okay. I will explain everything to you, I promise, but for now, you have to trust me and do as I say, exactly as I say, immediately."

"But, Mommy, I—"

"Gracie, please!"

Gracie nodded and opened her door, then grabbed the bag from the floor.

Shae walked beside her into the house and paused to listen in the doorway. Silence. "Go, now."

She lifted the phone on her way through the kitchen and followed Gracie to her room. Everything seemed to be in order. Even though she knew she wasn't handling the situation well, she couldn't seem to get her emotions under control. For years she'd kept to herself and worked as an IT tech from home, but then Gracie had started school and wanted to play sports, make friends, sing in the church choir. Shae should have known better. And now her daughter was in danger because Shae hadn't kept a low enough profile.

She dialed the number, listened to it ring…and ring. That wasn't right. Someone was supposed to be available at all times in case of an emergency, in case she was discovered. She disconnected and tried again. Nothing. Her breath came in shallow gasps. It would be okay. She'd contemplated not calling anyway, so maybe it was for the best no one answered. Maybe God was leading her elsewhere.

She hurried to Gracie's bedroom to check on her, and her heart shattered when her daughter picked up the stuffed bunny she'd stopped sleeping with a year ago and hugged it close as she filled her bag with her most prized possessions.

Shae left her to it and went to her own room. She grabbed the two flight bags, dug through one for the handgun, took the bullets from the locked safe in her closet and loaded the weapon. Then she stuck it into the waistband of her shorts and shrugged a sweatshirt over it before dropping the bags beside the door to the garage. All of her important documents were already stashed in waterproof cases inside the waterproof bag, as well as a good amount of cash she'd saved over the years. "Gracie, let's go."

Gracie emerged from the hallway, her bag and Mr. Cuddles clutched against her chest.

"Oh, baby, I—"

A car door slammed right outside the house, cutting her off.

"Get down. Hide. Now! And remember cheesemonkey. Every single thing we practiced."

Gracie scrambled beneath the Christmas tree in the corner, trampling packages, then peered between the branches.

Shae grabbed a pen and paper from her desk, scribbled the phone number down, and shoved the paper into Gracie's hand. With no time for more than a quick reassurance, Shae backed toward the door. "If anything happens to me, you run to Katie's house. Do you understand me?"

The doorbell rang.

Gracie's gaze shot to the door and she nodded, teeth chattering, eyes wide.

"When you get there…" Three houses down with two possible killers on her heels. And now she was bringing this mess onto someone else, someone who had only ever been kind to them, who'd become a friend. "You hide until Miss Reva gets home, then tell her to call that number and tell whoever answers what happened. She should tell them who you are and that you need help. Okay?"

"Uh…huh…"

An insistent pounding rattled the front door. "Avery!"

Shae's blood ran to ice as she stared deeply into her daughter's brilliant blue eyes, then yanked the handgun from her waistband. No one should know that name. She'd shed it six years ago when she'd become Shae Evans. "Get down!"

Despite her shocked expression when she caught sight of the weapon, Gracie crouched lower.

Hand shaking wildly, Shae aimed the gun at the door just as it splintered beneath a forceful kick.

Mason Payne kicked Avery Bennett's front door again. No. Wait. No longer Avery—she was Shae now, Shae Evans. He had to remember that.

He pressed his ear against the door and listened for any sound, praying he'd made it in time to save her. Her handler had been killed close by in what was no accident, considering her brake line had been cut. He could only conclude she'd been trying to reach Shae and that her cover had been blown.

Either way, whether Shae forgave him for walking

away from her six years ago or not, he was going to have to convince her to let him get her to a safe house. If she was half as stubborn as he remembered, he had a battle ahead of him. That was okay, though. He'd fight whatever battle it took to see her safe, and then he'd leave her in peace and continue his mission.

The door splintered beneath his next kick. He reached through the hole he'd made, unlocked the dead bolt and shoved the door open, weapon drawn.

And there she stood, like a warrior, every bit as beautiful and courageous as he remembered her. Long, dark hair hung in waves, framing a determined expression. Eyes the color of cocoa and wide with fear stared back at him, hands shaking as she aimed a handgun directly at his head. She took his breath away.

He stood perfectly still, removed his finger from the trigger of his own weapon and slowly lifted his hands as the six years since he'd last seen her melted away as if no time had passed. He shouldn't have left, should have at least tried to explain the guilt that had tortured him over his partner's death, the pain he'd felt that one of his own associates could have betrayed them…betrayed Shae. He should have been honest that Zac Jameson had come to him with information that Shae was still in danger, should have told her he was going to try to infiltrate the Kincaid organization in an effort to keep her safe.

But instead, Mason had gone undercover with Jameson Investigations, obsessed with getting to the truth, no matter the cost. And later, when he realized he probably wasn't going to find the answers he sought, he'd maintained his undercover identity to at least help those he could.

"Av— Uh… I mean, Shae." Nothing could have prepared him for the tidal wave of emotion the sight of her would evoke. He'd thought he'd mastered his feelings, had turned them off somewhere along the line in an effort to immerse himself in his undercover persona, but now the weight of them threatened to crush him. He inhaled and ruthlessly shoved everything aside—he had to if he was going to save her. He took a step toward her, needing to gain her trust again somehow, and quickly. No easy task, if the suspicion marring her expression was any indication. "Please, there's no time to explain. I need you to lower the weapon and come with me."

"M-Mason?" Her voice shook, the question more of a *what are you doing here* than a lack of recognition, though he'd certainly changed in the years since she'd last seen him.

Instead of the short, regulation haircut she'd remember, he now boasted a tail, tied at his nape and hanging between his shoulder blades. And where he'd always been clean-shaven, his undercover persona carefully maintained a five o'clock shadow. There had been no time to change his appearance once he'd found out she was in danger. Besides, he was going to have to go back under once he saw her to safety. "Yeah."

"What are you doing here? What happened to you? Wh-where have you been?"

"I'll explain everything, I promise, but there's no time right now. We have to get out of here." He took another step toward her, then froze when she gripped the weapon tighter and took a step back. "Shae, please."

Her gaze shifted past him, and he whirled to check for threats. And stopped short when he spotted a little girl peering back at him from behind a Christmas tree trimmed with colorful homemade ornaments. She couldn't be more than four or five...

Agony plowed into his chest. He tried to suck in a breath but couldn't. Mason had thought he couldn't feel any more than when he'd lain eyes on Shae again, but the sight of the child sent waves of pain crashing through him, along with a myriad of other emotions he couldn't even begin to comprehend, never mind name. Because that child was the spitting image of her mother, except for one telling feature—his own electric-blue eyes staring back at him.

She had to be his daughter. But she couldn't be. How could he not have known about her?

"Shae, I..." What could he say? He'd abandoned her while she'd carried his child. What kind of man would do that? But he hadn't known. He'd taken off right after the night they'd spent together, a reckless moment of celebrating life after everything had gone so horribly out of control. If he had known about the child, would he have left?

"Mason..." Tears tracked down Shae's cheeks.

Tires squealed, entirely too close, and dragged him back to reality. He peered out the door as a silver sedan rounded the corner and barreled toward them. "All right... It's all right. We have to go. Now!"

Shae was already moving. She grabbed two bags from beside the door. "Gracie, grab your bag. Hurry. Cheese-monkey."

A nickname? No, a code word. Shae was savvy as ever. The little girl sobbed softly as she hugged a bag and what looked like a stuffed rabbit against her. Recognition almost drove him to his knees. He remembered the rabbit with the big floppy ears, had picked it up in the hospital gift shop and given it to Shae the night before he'd left her, the night he'd been betrayed, the night his partner had been killed. Had he known even then that he was going to leave? Had he planned all along to go undercover in search of answers?

Shae hustled Gracie past him.

He had to get himself together. "Wait!"

She stopped dead in her tracks and stepped in front of her daughter. His daughter?

The sedan skidded to a stop in front of the house. It was too late to make it to his vehicle parked out front. "Where's your car?"

"In the garage."

"Go." He gestured with his gun, away from the front door, then followed as she ran through the kitchen and into the garage.

She flung the car's back door open and threw her bags on the floor as Gracie climbed in, then strapped her into the booster seat and slammed the door shut behind her daughter, hopped into the passenger seat and buckled her seat belt.

Mason slid behind the wheel. "Do you have a remote in the car?"

She flipped the driver's side visor down to show him.

He shifted into Reverse and hit the button. "Get down."

Gracie hunched as low as she could in the seat, and Shae slid down in the passenger seat and peered out the side window.

He slammed on the gas the instant the garage door rose high enough to clear the car's roof.

"They're coming." Shae braced herself against the dashboard. "They have guns."

The car rocked as he barely slowed to shift into Drive, then punched it. The tires spun, then gripped and shot the car forward. "Hold on."

He'd have only seconds to lose their attackers. If they reached the vehicle before he could get out of sight, they'd be harder to shake. He didn't recognize the two men, but that didn't mean anything. Mason had infiltrated the Kincaid organization six years ago, after its leader, Quentin Kincaid, had gone to prison—thanks to Shae's testimony. She'd been Kincaid's personal assistant, at least for the legal front of his business, and when she'd realized what other business he was in, she'd used her access to uncover a treasure trove of information the feds used to bury him.

But even from prison, he was in charge, using his fairly incompetent son, Sebastian, as a puppet to continue running the family business. While Mason had managed to have many of their lower-level thugs arrested and convicted, he'd never been able to make it to the top. If these were upper-level hit men, he wouldn't know them, and Shae was in even more trouble than he'd thought. On a brighter note, if he didn't know them, they wouldn't know him, either, and his cover wouldn't be compromised.

He skidded around a corner, fishtailed and regained control.

"They're following." Shae swiped at the tears on her cheeks.

A quick glance in the rearview mirror told him they weren't going to make it out of there without a chase. So be it. He pressed down on the gas pedal, increasing his already reckless speed through the residential neighborhood's narrow streets, and took another corner practically on two wheels.

The vehicle behind them sped up and closed in.

Mason hit the brakes.

Gracie squealed.

"Hold on to something!" He hit the gas again, lurching forward as the car in pursuit slowed.

Shae shifted up higher in her seat, grabbed the handle above the door, and looked over her shoulder. "Gracie, hold on tight, baby."

"Mommy?"

"It's okay, honey. I'll explain everything once we get somewhere safe." She looked at Mason, chewed on her lower lip for a moment, then seemed to make up her mind. "This is Mason, and he'll keep us safe. If anything happens to me, you listen to him. Understand?"

"Uh...huh." The little girl started to cry, and the soft sobs tore at Mason's heart.

He wanted desperately to pull over, to reassure her he'd keep her safe, to meet the daughter he'd never known existed until moments ago. *Daughter.* The word sounded so foreign in his mind. And yet, he'd apparently been a father for years. He just couldn't wrap his head around it. Instead, he kept one eye firmly riveted to the road in front of them and the other on the rear-view mirror.

Shae reached back between the seats for her daughter.

Mason refrained from admonishing her, from telling her if he had to stop short, her arm would probably snap. The child clearly needed comfort, so he'd just have to be careful not to stop short. Fat chance, with their pursuers hugging his bumper.

"Watch out for the—"

He hit a speed table full on, jolting the car so hard his

teeth snapped closed on his tongue. The coppery taste of blood filled his mouth. He'd forgotten about them, and in the darkness, with the reflections of Christmas lights dotting the neighborhood, he hadn't seen it. "How many more?"

"Uh…" Shae closed her eyes and mumbled something that sounded like counting under her breath. "There's a total of four along the main road out of the development, so three more."

"Hold on." He clamped his teeth together to keep from biting his tongue again but didn't slow when he came to the next one. Instead, at the last minute, he skirted around it on someone's lawn, barely missing a blow-up reindeer and losing precious seconds. Did it matter, though? He wasn't going to lose their pursuers inside the development, nor was he going to stop and give them the opportunity to attack. Considering the situation, they were pretty much at a stalemate. Cars parked along the narrow streets and the occasional car driving in the opposite direction kept them from flanking him, so he slowed for the next two speed tables.

The driver behind him did the same.

Mason barely eased off the gas as he hooked a right turn out of the development, not because he had any clue where he was going but to keep from having to wait for traffic. He accelerated, passed two cars on the left and barely missed clipping the bumper of the car in front as he nipped back into the lane just in time to avoid a head-on collision.

Hindered by oncoming traffic, his pursuers bounced along the shoulder as they passed the same two cars on the right then tried to inch alongside him.

He swerved, tapping their car and forcing them to back off or tumble into the swampy ditch bordering the road. "They're not going to stop chasing us, and they have no regard for civilian casualties. Is there a more isolated road around here? Somewhere with less traffic and less chance for collateral damage?"

Gracie whimpered from the back seat.

Mason pushed the sound out of his mind. He had to if he was going to think clearly. He needed an open stretch to increase his lead, then some way to ditch them.

"Make the next right. If you take that all the way to the end, it turns into a dirt road."

A dirt road was risky—too dry and he'd be more likely to lose control and spin out, too wet and he could easily get stuck in the muck. "What else?"

She looked at him, held his gaze for the instant he could take his eyes off the road and shook her head. "Any other direction and we're headed into either residential developments, some of which only have one way in and out, or commercial areas with traffic lights at every intersection."

Since their pursuers had no problem driving recklessly, he assumed they wouldn't blink twice at walking up to the car at a stoplight and shooting all three of them. That was Kincaid's style. And if they worked for Sebastian Kincaid, as he suspected, they'd never risk his wrath by returning empty-handed after a hit had been ordered. Quentin was ruthless, but his son was another matter entirely. In addition to being incompetent, the man was mercilessly cruel, seemed to enjoy hurting others in the most brutal manner he could devise. Sebastian was a weapon Quentin Kincaid aimed at anyone who crossed him. It was one of the reasons Mason had never made lieutenant—while he'd been willing to do enough to maintain his cover, he couldn't condone what would be required to move up in the organization. The dirt road began to look more appealing.

He hit the brakes, spun the wheel to the right and took the turn. He fumbled his cell phone out of his pocket and glanced at it long enough to dial the most recent number.

Zac Jameson picked up halfway through the first ring. "Did you get to her?"

"I have her, but we're in trouble."

"Where?"

With a dead calm he didn't feel, despite years of practice, Mason relayed their position and the direction they were headed.

"Sending backup." And with that, Zac disconnected.

"Who was that?" Shae stared at him, her eyes filled with a distrust that served as a reminder of how horribly he'd failed her, failed their child.

But what could he have been to either of them? A man so engrossed in his own vendetta he'd had nothing left to give? They'd probably been better off without him. Until they'd been found, of course.

"Zac Jameson. I've worked with him for years, and he's a friend."

"I hope he's a better friend than the last one you trusted."

The words struck their target like an arrow straight through his heart. "I'm sorry, Shae. I don't know what else to say, except to promise I'll keep you safe. Both of you. I'll tell you everything, but I need you to trust me right now so we can get out of this mess."

She checked the side-view mirror, glanced at Gracie trembling in her booster seat, then dropped her head back and sighed. "I'm sorry, Mason. That was uncalled-for."

"But true enough, so don't worry about it." He hit the dirt road, only sliding a little, then increased his speed.

Shae closed her eyes and surprised him by mumbling a prayer. He hadn't remembered her sharing his own faith, so strong back then, before betrayal and death had hardened him, waning the longer he'd been undercover without finding answers. Perhaps it was time to turn back to it.

Metal crunched against metal as their pursuers slammed their back end, shoving them forward.

Mason increased his speed. Marshy land and murky water bordered them on both sides, cypress trees dotted the water's edge and underbrush grew thicker as they moved deeper into the swamp. Black clouds gathered, darkening the already pitch-black night as the storms Zac had warned him of moved closer. They had some time left, but not much.

Shae braced her hands against the dashboard. "You have to slow for the bridge."

"Where?"

"About a mile from here. An old wooden bridge."

"Is there any other way around?"

"No."

Kicking himself would do no good. He'd barely had time to reach Shae after he'd found out she was in trouble, hadn't been able to scope the area in search of an escape route. Now, he'd just have to make the best of the situation and hope Zac got help to them in time.

He rounded a curve, and the bridge, if you could call it that, loomed ahead of him. The wooden structure had seen better days. The railings had long ago begun to rot, probably along with most of the other boards. Shae was right; he would have to slow down.

He checked the rearview mirror. Their pursuers still clung like glue, but they'd eased off a little, no doubt assuming he'd made a mistake heading into the swamp and they'd have time to come alongside them if and when the narrow road widened.

The joints creaked and moaned as he hit the bridge too fast, bounced, then slammed on his brakes when another vehicle skidded to a stop, blocking the far end of the bridge. Hope tried to flare, but he tamped it down quickly enough. If Zac's help had reached them, they'd have waited until after Mason crossed before blocking the bridge.

They were trapped.

He slammed the shifter into Reverse, twisted around to see behind him and hit the gas.

The other driver accelerated in a game of chicken Mason had no hope of winning.

Mason tried to maneuver around him on the narrow structure, might even have made it if their pursuer hadn't yanked the wheel at the last minute and hit them from the side.

Mason's head cracked hard against the driver's side window as they spun. Darkness encroached in his peripheral vision. The car hit the railing. With one loud groan, the rail gave way and they were airborne, plunging toward the black water below.

TWO

The airbag exploded in Shae's face, and she struggled to free herself, check on Gracie and get to her weapon all at once. Their attackers would stand above them on the bridge, making it easy to pick them off as they emerged from the vehicle. "Gracie?"

"M-M-Mommy?" The whisper was soft and shaky, but at least she was alive.

Now, if she could just get her out of there without anyone getting shot. "Are you hurt, honey?"

Gracie's harsh breaths echoed in the car. She sniffed. "My heart hurts, 'cause I'm afraid."

"Okay. It's okay, baby. Listen to me…" A glance at Mason made her blood run cold. His eyes were closed, head lolling at an unnatural angle. The realization that she still felt something for him hit her like a physical blow. But she had no time to reflect on it now. "Can you open your seat belt?"

Even as she asked, she reached for her own and found it stuck. A knife? Did she have one in the car? No. Maybe in one of the flight bags—she couldn't remember. "Mason?"

"Okay, I got it off." Gracie slid forward and caught herself against the two front seats. "Now what?"

Pain pounded in Shae's head, stealing her focus, making it difficult to think straight. Her ears rang viciously, drowning out any possible sounds of pursuit. She couldn't think…needed to. If they didn't get out of there, they were as good as dead. Mason…she had to wake him, shouldn't move him. But what else could she do? She couldn't leave him there. If she could even free herself from the harness. "Gracie, in the front compartment of one of my bags, there should be a knife. It's folded up. Find it, but do not open it."

She closed her eyes and held her breath for a moment, listened past Gracie's soft whimpers and rummaging, and heard Mason's ragged breathing. A wave of dizziness overtook her, and her stomach heaved. She choked down the bile surging up her throat. "Mason, you've got to wake up. We have to get out of here."

"Here, Mommy." Gracie handed her the knife, and she opened it and cut her own seat belt free.

The pressure of the lake water against the doors would probably keep them from opening. With that in mind, she opened her window. "Gracie, we have to get out my side of the car before the windows are below the waterline. Can you slide over and open your window?"

"Oh-kay."

Shae hit the mechanism on Mason's belt, and the clasp slid free. As soon as Gracie's window opened fully, she reached across Mason and shut off the headlights and the ignition. No sense announcing their location to any sniper who might be lying in wait on the bridge.

"Are we getting out into the water?" Gracie's voice was barely more than a whisper.

"Yes."

"But it's dark out. What if there are snakes? Or gators? Or…" She sucked in frantic breaths and started to hyperventilate.

"Gracie, stop! You have to calm down." Shae held Mason tight against the seat to keep him from falling forward and hitting his face against the dashboard, which had pushed into the passenger compartment on impact. Gracie needed something to concentrate on other than the danger they faced from the swamp and the gunmen who were likely waiting on the bridge for them. Their best hope would be to get out quietly and pray their attackers couldn't see them in the dark. "I need your help."

"Uh…huh…okay." Tremors shook her voice, and she continued to cry, but she seemed to have regained some semblance of control. "What do I have to do?"

"Help me hold Mason against the seat so I can see how badly he's hurt."

The request brought a fresh wave of tears. "Is…is… he gonna die?"

"No," Shae said firmly. She wouldn't accept that, couldn't face the fact that, in another moment, she'd have to leave him there at the mercy of the gunmen. She turned, and water sloshed around her feet. They were sinking. She staved off the panic. One problem at a time. "Mason, wake up. Now! We can't stay here. We need to move."

Next to Gracie's whimpers, his soft groan was the sweetest sound she'd ever heard.

Oh, God, please help us. Help me get Gracie and Mason out of here, and help me get them to safety. Please, please, please… She repeated the plea over and over in her head. "Mason."

He lifted his head, eyes rolling once as he struggled to focus on her.

"Mason, please, wake up. They're going to find us. We have to get out of here."

Blood flowed down the side of his face.

"Gracie, give me a shirt or something out of one of the bags."

She yanked out a tank top and handed it to Shae.

Leaving it folded, Shae pressed it against Mason's wound. "Can you hear me?"

"What?" His head fell back, and he squinted out the front windshield, where nothing but blackness was visible, then lurched upright and braced himself against the steering wheel.

"We went off the bridge into the swamp. The two men who were following us are out there, plus however many more were in the second vehicle blocking the other side of the bridge. We have to move."

Coming halfway to his senses, Mason sat up straighter and patted the holster on his hip. "Where's my gun?"

"I don't know, but I have mine."

"Okay. All right." He squeezed his eyes closed then opened them a moment later. "We have to get the windows open."

"Mine already is."

"I'm mixed up. Where is the bridge?"

"To your left. We need to go out my side."

"Okay. You go first, then I'll get Gracie out to you and follow."

She had little trust that he could manage to get himself out of the car, never mind Gracie, but there was no time to argue or delay. They'd waited too long already.

"Keep your head below the roof line."

"Okay." She tucked the weapon into her waistband, then half climbed, half slid out the window into the chilly water, careful to keep her head low and stay far enough from the car that it didn't pull her under as it slowly sank. Without a sound, she treaded water and held her arms out to Gracie, who wrapped her arms around Shae's neck and wiggled out the back window.

When she hit the water, she hissed through her teeth and squeezed tight enough to cut off Shae's supply of the reeking, thick air. It was almost a relief.

She pressed her mouth against Gracie's ear, struggling to stay afloat with her daughter in her arms. "Hold on to me, but loosen your arms a little."

She nodded, teeth chattering, no doubt more from fear than the water that held only a slight chill, and wrapped her legs around Shae's waist. Her iron grip around Shae's neck eased a little.

Mason emerged and gestured her toward the far side of the lake, into the marshy wetlands.

Gunshots split the night, followed by three muffled plops as the bullets hit the water—far too close for comfort.

Gracie gasped and opened her mouth to scream, but Mason clamped a hand over her face.

Shae turned slowly and aimed her weapon toward the men illuminated in the headlights of their vehicles atop the bridge.

Mason laid a hand over the weapon, pushing it down, and shook his head. He placed his finger against his lips to shush both Shae and Gracie and slid lower into the water.

Shae followed.

Gracie clung tighter as Shae resisted the urge to rush. The more they stirred the water, the easier they'd be to locate. Full darkness had already fallen over the swamp, not even lit by the moon or stars as thick cloud cover from the coming storms blocked their light.

A few more shots rang out but found targets closer to the bridge. Their attackers must be assuming they would try for the closest shore, but instead, they swam toward the far shore, deeper into the swamp.

She had to assume the men would figure it out and follow them. Or call in whatever expert trackers and equipment they'd need to locate Shae and Gracie in the swamp. The Kincaid organization had the funds, and they could afford to wait.

Well, that was fine. It would give her, Gracie and Mason a chance to get away.

After what felt like hours but probably wasn't more than twenty minutes, she rolled onto her back, floating for a moment with her daughter lying on top of her. Between the airbag hitting her full force and having to swim while holding Gracie, Shae's chest screamed in protest.

Mason paused, treading water and resting a reassuring hand on her shoulder. Then they pressed on. She breathed a sigh of relief when her feet hit the gross bottom and she gained her footing as it began to slope upward.

Clutching Gracie tightly, Shae staggered onto the shore. She kept low, hoping their pursuers wouldn't be able to see where they'd left the lake and entered the forest.

Mason crouched down, looking toward the bridge, then urged her forward into the thick vegetation.

Everything in Shae begged her to stay where it was relatively clear, where they could see any threats nature might throw at them as their eyes adjusted to the darkness. But she did as he indicated and crept into the dense foliage with Gracie clinging tight. Who knew? Maybe they were better off not knowing what was out there. Although Shae liked living in Florida, enjoyed the year-round warmth and sunshine after spending her whole life suffering New York's cold, gray winters, she'd never been able to rid herself of the mind-numbing fear of coming face-to-face with some of the region's more deadly creatures.

She stumbled over a thick root and went down hard on one knee, biting back a cry. Then held her breath and listened to see if she'd given their position away.

Gracie snuggled against her, getting as close as possible.

It was only then that Shae realized she was still clutching Mr. Cuddles as tightly as Shae clung to her weapon. Tears threatened.

Mason leaned over them, using his body as a shield. "Are you hurt?"

Swallowing the lump in her throat, Shae shook her head.

"We have to keep moving." He glanced over his shoulder. "We've got a head start, but as soon as they get someone with an airboat and spotlights in here, we're done."

Shae nodded and struggled to her feet.

Mason slid an arm around her and helped her up as she set Gracie down beside her. He moved so the little girl was positioned between them, then pointed in the direction he wanted her to go. As they walked, Gracie hugged her bunny and clung tightly to Shae's hand, careful to stay between Shae and Mason.

What must Mason be thinking? There was no doubt in her mind he'd realized Gracie was his daughter. She'd seen that punch of recognition, followed by the instant of shock. And then he'd shut everything down, his expression going hard, his eyes unreadable. Did he blame Shae for not letting him know about her? But how could she have? She'd had no idea where to find him. Besides, Maria Delarosa had known about Gracie, and surely they'd had some contact. How else would he have known where to find her? But he'd seemed so surprised. No, he hadn't known. Of that she was certain.

So, what was going through his mind?

"Freeze!" Mason hissed, dragging her from distractions better left for a more appropriate time— or, even better, never.

Shae stopped and listened intently for whatever had put him on alert.

"Don't move." Even as he said it, he inched in front of them.

Movement caught Shae's attention, shadows flickering in the dark all around their feet, substantial, disturbed by the intrusion through their world. "What are they—"

But before she even finished the question, she realized what they were…baby alligators. Tons of them, wriggling and squirming in their muddy nest. She fought desperately against the fear threatening to paralyze her.

Standing in front of Gracie and Shae, Mason started to guide them slowly backward, retracing their steps away from the gator nest.

A low growl came from somewhere in the dark.

Shae fought the urge to lift her child into her arms, to turn and run full speed in the opposite direction, to flee back toward their pursuers who, at the moment, seemed like the less dangerous threat.

Mason extended his arms, sidestepping farther in front of Shae and Gracie, once again shielding them, placing himself between them and danger. At least she had no doubt that no matter what he thought of the fact he had a child, he would give his life to see her safe.

Another bellow sounded as something huge crashed through the brush.

There was no time to run, no time to think, only a split second to react. Keeping the eight-foot gator sprinting toward him in his peripheral vision, Mason spun around, lifted Gracie and flung her aside, and hissed, "Go, run."

Shae backed up, slid on the mud and went down hard on her bottom.

The alligator, either sensing the easier prey or seeing Shae as more of a threat to its offspring, shifted its attention from Mason and set its sights on her. When it charged, Mason kicked it hard in the side, and it whirled on him. He jumped back toward the lake to draw the gator away and give Shae and Gracie time to run deeper into the forest. The jaws clamped shut inches from his leg, then it swung back and caught him in the shin with its massive head. He went down, rolled and surged to his feet in hip-deep water.

He'd spent enough time numbing his mind in front of the Nature Channel to know he didn't want to fight a gator in the water, where it would have the advantage. Seemed ironic—all those nights spent wallowing in guilt might now save him. He surged toward land, desperate to get there before the animal attacked. The gator charged again, and he dived over it, landed hard on his hip and shoulder, then rolled back toward the not-so-dry land and scrambled to his feet. He slid as he struggled to gain purchase in the muck.

Where were Shae and Gracie? He'd lost track of them but didn't dare take his gaze off the predator hoping to make a midnight snack of him. Returning to land had brought him closer to the nest, further agitating the creature. The blood pouring down the side of his face from where his head had hit the window probably wasn't helping matters.

The gator barreled toward him again, hissing wildly. For such a large, heavy reptile, it moved incredibly fast. But only in short bursts, if he remembered correctly.

He knew he should run, not in a zigzag pattern but a full-out sprint in a straight line, hoping the gator would tire before it could catch him. But he couldn't do that, not without knowing where Shae and Gracie had gone. He didn't dare call out. The gator wasn't the only thing stalking them in the night—might not even be the most dangerous. If they could just get away from the nest, it would probably leave them be.

He caught movement in his peripheral vision. Shae appeared in the small clearing with a long branch. She prodded the creature, dragging its attention from Mason.

The instant it turned toward Shae, Mason dived onto its back, squeezed tightly with his legs and covered its eyes with his hand, forcing its head down. Then he freed one hand and clamped it over the gator's mouth, holding it closed. While alligators could snap their mouths closed with incredible force, they couldn't open them with equal strength. That much he remembered from wildlife documentaries he'd seen, while he'd silently marveled, from the safety of his couch, why anyone would willingly wrestle such a large and dangerous creature.

The gator tried to roll, a death roll if Mason couldn't hold on, if the creature got hold of him, if it got him into the water.

Mason extended one leg, dug deep into the silt. No way could he let it turn over or he'd lose his precarious hold. When it stilled, he chanced a quick glance at Shae, still holding the stick and watching warily. He didn't dare risk more than the slightest whisper. "Where's Gracie?"

"Over there." She gestured behind her toward the deeper forest.

"Safe?"

"Yes."

The gator bucked and squirmed.

"Okay, back off. I'm going to try to get off her and get out of here."

She nodded, backed up and hefted the stick higher, as if ready to strike.

He waited again for the gator to still, then shoved off, jumping backward to his feet, and braced for attack. When it remained motionless, attention still focused on Shae, he skirted around it, waded slowly into the shallow water to keep from moving closer to the nest and turned to face it as he backed toward Shae.

"Go," he whispered to her.

The alligator watched him a few moments more, then

turned and lumbered back toward her nest. Mason finally exhaled the breath he'd been holding. As he followed Shae deeper into the woods, muscles he didn't know he had screamed in protest. He used the back of his wrist to wipe the blood away from his eye. Throbbing pain in his shin, where the gator's head had connected, forced him to limp, slowing his progress.

When he caught up to her, he asked, "Are you hurt?"

"I'm okay."

"Shae." He reached for her, gripped her arm and turned her to face him, running his gaze over every inch of her. "Are you hurt?"

She shook her head. "A few bumps and bruises. Nothing serious."

"Okay. What about Gracie?" He released her and resumed walking next to her.

"She twisted her ankle. I'm not sure she can walk."

He picked up his pace, the sudden need to reach the child who was hiding alone in the swamp, no doubt terrified, too overwhelming to ignore. "Do you still have your gun?"

"Yeah."

And yet she'd come to his aid carrying a large stick instead of the deadly weapon. "Why didn't you shoot the gator?"

Her gaze flicked to him, and she frowned.

"I'm not criticizing, just curious."

She studied him another moment then shrugged. "I couldn't get a shot with you in the way."

Yet there'd been times he'd backed off. "And?"

"And I didn't want to risk those men hearing the gunshots and finding us." She averted her gaze.

"Good thinking." He would have had the same thoughts under the circumstances. But there was something more, something unspoken she obviously didn't feel comfortable sharing with him. Maybe this could be his first push toward gaining her trust, because they weren't going to survive this night if he couldn't. "What else?"

She sighed, and her shoulders slumped a bit. "I wouldn't have let it kill you, or hurt you, but you seemed to be holding your own, so…"

He waited her out, but as he thought of Gracie hiding in the woods, alone with no one to protect her, he figured he already knew.

"It was the babies. I couldn't take their mother, couldn't stand the thought of leaving them alone out here when she'd done nothing but come to their defense." She swiped her palms over her cheeks. "I'll do whatever it takes to protect my daughter, to protect you, even to survive, but I won't ever take an innocent life."

My daughter. It was the perfect opening, the perfect opportunity to ask, "Don't you mean *our* daughter," to confirm what he suspected—what he knew. Instead, he remained silent. *Coward.*

They reached Gracie, curled in a small ball beneath a rotting tree that had long ago fallen. She was hugging the stuffed rabbit.

Shae pulled the little girl into her arms. "It's okay, honey. I'm here now."

Gracie wrapped her arms and legs around her mother and clung so tight Mason feared she'd never let go. Then she buried her face into Shae's shoulder and cried.

Shae cradled and rocked her and whispered softly in her ear.

As much as he hated to intrude on the moment, they had to move. The noise they'd made fighting the gator could well have drawn the attention of their pursuers. He listened but didn't hear anything to indicate they were being followed. Still, he didn't dare waste what precious lead time they had. "We have to go."

Shae glared at him over Gracie's shoulder and rubbed circles on the girl's back.

"I'm sorry, Shae, but there's no choice. We've got to keep moving."

She held his gaze a moment longer, then sighed. "All right. I know. Gracie, honey, can you walk?"

She sniffed, wiped her face with the back of her hand and nodded.

When Shae lowered her to her feet, she took one step and cried out, then slapped a hand over her mouth. "I'm sorry."

"It's okay, honey. Shh…" Shae soothed as she lifted Gracie back into her arms. She looked at Mason. "I don't think it's broken but probably badly sprained."

He approached Gracie, not knowing what to say to her. He didn't have much—or any—experience with kids. Did she know he was her father? Had she recognized him the same way he'd recognized her? What had Shae told her about him? What could this child think of the man who'd abandoned her? "Gracie, is it all right if I take a look at your ankle?"

Keeping her head against Shae's shoulder, she turned to face him and nodded.

He couldn't see well enough in the darkness to tell if it was bruised, but there was definitely swelling. She couldn't walk, so she was going to have to be carried.

No matter how petite Gracie was, no way could Shae carry her all the way through the swamp, especially at night under thick cloud cover.

Thunder rumbled, deep and loud.

"Have you ever had a piggyback ride, Gracie?" He should know that, shouldn't he? Should have been there for that.

She nodded, teeth chattering.

Before he could check the instinct, he reached out to her—couldn't help himself—and tucked her long, dark hair, now matted with dirt and muck, behind her ears. "If Mom helps you onto my back, I can carry you for a bit."

She looked at her mother. A flash of lightning illuminated the terror reflected in her eyes.

Shae wiped tears from her daughter's face. "It's okay. We have to move. You understand that, honey."

She nodded, sucked in a breath and straightened.

Mason turned so Shae could help her onto his back. She was wet and cold, and he shifted her more snugly against him.

When Gracie wrapped her thin arms tightly around his neck, a kind of fear he'd never felt before rushed through him. This child, so small, so delicate, so fragile, was his responsibility, his to protect. He hooked his arms beneath her legs and boosted her higher, then started forward. He'd faced the irate alligator with less apprehension than he did his own daughter.

Then another thought struck. What if Shae wouldn't allow him to be a part of Gracie's life? Was that even what he wanted? The idea that he'd even consider it startled him. He'd never thought about being a dad. Kincaid's trial had lasted more than a year, and while he and Shae had been together through most of that time, had even discussed him leaving the FBI to go into witness protection with her, they'd never discussed having children.

Then, after he'd had to leave her to go undercover, he hadn't allowed himself to feel anything. He'd given up all of his hopes and dreams, given up everything but the determination to take down Kincaid's organization and save as many people as possible until he could do so.

So, what now? Did he want to take on all the responsibilities of fatherhood? Would Gracie even accept him as her father after five years without him?

And how selfish was he to want to be in her life? He was in deep over his head in a criminal organization, undercover for close to six years. What would happen when Sebastian Kincaid found out the truth? He'd send assassins after him, just as he had Shae. The kindest thing he could do for both Shae and her daughter would be to see them safe and then distance himself. Besides, he had to go back undercover as soon as they were safe, so whatever he might or might not feel or want was irrelevant anyway.

Two fat raindrops dropped onto his face, and then the sky opened up and dumped gallons all at once.

When he glanced at Shae, she looked back at him, and a smiled played at the corners of her mouth. She shook her head and laughed quietly, a sound he hadn't heard in so long. Then she sighed and lifted her face to the rain.

It struck him, in that moment, how beautiful she was, both inside and out. He'd admired that about her, the way she could find happiness in the simplest moments, be grateful for even the smallest blessings. That ability to recognize and revel in the joys life brought was a skill that had always eluded him. He could also admit he admired her courage in the face of danger, the way she could find, if not humor, then irony in any situation. That was one of the things he loved most about—

Yikes! Whoa. Hit the brakes, buddy. Everything in him went still. Love? The feeling had crept up on him, surprised him. He might once have loved Avery Bennett, but that was a long time ago, and a lot had happened since that time. Too much. He was no longer the man he'd been six years ago, could no longer feel love… or pain. He'd completely detached himself from everything he'd ever known. And Avery no longer existed. He'd lost her on that long-ago night, along with his partner and whichever friend had betrayed him and stolen his ability to trust. Shae Evans was a stranger to him, just as he must be to her.

He shook off whatever emotions had begun to creep up and blindside him, probably due to the head injury he'd sustained and the waning adrenaline rush from fighting the gator. Everyone would be better off if he could keep his head in the game, because more than one gator lurked in the swamp. Aside from the human killers on their tails, the night was filled with gators, water moccasins and other venomous snakes, bears, wild boars, and panthers—all no doubt scenting the blood flowing from his head wound. And then there was the quicksand. Even if their attackers never found them, there was a better-than-good chance they'd never make it out of the swamp alive.

THREE

When the rain eased up, Shae stopped walking, bent and propped her hands on her knees. She just needed a moment to catch her breath. Once she had, she straightened, then simply stood, staring at the ground.

Mason stopped beside her and waited, diligently scanning the woods in every direction.

The slow swim from the half-submerged car had soaked them, and the rain had made things worse. Shae's clothing felt heavy, like it was dragging her down. Mud, along with a bunch of other muck she didn't dare think about, caked her sneakers and legs. Her muscles screamed in pain, her chest ached from the crash, begging her to slow down, and exhaustion beat at her. And the rain would start up again soon enough as the next storm sought them out.

Mason didn't appear to be in much better shape. Though he carried Gracie on his back without complaint, his limp had increased over the past few minutes, and his pace had slowed considerably.

Plus, they had absolutely no idea where they were headed. The thick clouds blocked the moon and stars, and no lights were visible in any direction to indicate a sign of civilization.

She rested a hand on Gracie's back, feeling each tremor that shook her little girl's delicate frame, and turned to Mason. "We have to stop."

He glanced in the direction they'd come from and tilted his head, as if listening.

"I haven't heard anyone following us." And she'd been tracking the sounds around them for the past few minutes. "We can't keep going, Mason. We all need to rest. Besides, we have no clue where we're headed. For all we know, we could have circled around and be walking straight into a trap. Or we might walk so far into the swamp we can't find our way back out. With all this rain, and more on the way, it's going to start flooding."

He nodded. "I've been thinking the same, but we need higher ground and some kind of shelter, and we can't stray too far from the lake. It's the main landmark we can use as a reference."

He didn't have to tell her that. The stretch of land they'd been walking on had turned spongier, sucking at her shoes each time she took a step.

He hefted Gracie up higher, and she lifted her head. "Can we go home now? Please?"

Shae's heart ached for her, and she reached out to cup Gracie's cheek. She was so frightened. The only life she'd ever known had been filled with joy and love and fun. She wasn't equipped to handle this kind of trauma—though she'd held up well enough so far. Maybe she was stronger than Shae realized. She hoped so, considering they had a long journey ahead of them, both out of the swamp and to a whole new life. She didn't relish having to tell Gracie they could never return to the life she'd known, that even if they could escape their stalkers, they'd have to start over somewhere new, with new identities, new names. She could only deal with one crisis at a time. "It's okay, honey. For now, though, we're going to have an adventure. Okay?"

"I don't like having an adventure." Pouting, she lowered her head against Mason.

"I know, baby. I know." She rubbed her daughter's back, trying her best to soothe her. Tears threatened, but she fought them. The last thing Gracie needed was her mother falling apart. But Shae needed quiet, needed peace and time to reflect and pray, to decide what to do and where to go from there—assuming they made it through the night.

She slid her hand to the back of Gracie's head, pressing her forehead against her daughter's. "We have no choice, Gracie. Having a camp-out will be safer than walking in the dark when we don't know where we're going."

Gracie remained quiet for a moment, seeming to think the situation over. Then she nodded against Shae's head before straightening and gripping even tighter against Mason's back.

Mason frowned and looked around, then gave Gracie a bounce. "Hey, kiddo, can you pop down and stand right here and keep an eye on your mom for a few minutes while I see if I can find us a good campsite?"

Without saying anything, the little girl slid from his back and leaned against Shae's side.

Shae wrapped an arm around her shoulders and pulled her close. She was worried about her. It wasn't like Gracie to be so quiet, even if she was hurt. Gracie was an outgoing, athletic child who liked to play all kinds of games and sports, and when you played hard and with the passion for fun Gracie had, injuries came with the territory.

Mason squatted in front of her and gripped her hands. "Why don't you just think of this as a challenge, like in a book or a movie?"

Gracie shrugged, keeping her head down.

When Mason stood, he rubbed her head and squeezed Shae's arm. "I'll be back in a few minutes. If there's any problem, you have the gun. Don't hesitate to use it."

She nodded, grateful for everything he'd done for them as she watched him melt into the shadows. No matter what was going on and how she felt about him disappearing six years ago, he'd come back now, when they needed him the most, and he...

Wait... Why had he come back? How could he have known they were in danger? Shown up at the exact same moment as their attackers? Was it possible he'd kept tabs on her—on them—all along? Could he have known about his child all this time and said nothing?

No. No way. She'd seen the shock in his eyes when he'd spotted Gracie peeking out from behind the Christmas tree.

Christmas. It had to be past midnight at this point, which meant it was the twenty-fourth. Tonight would be Christmas Eve, the holiest night of the year. She thought of the presents she'd gotten Gracie, wrapped and tucked away in Shae's closet, to be put out after they'd gone to mass and Gracie had settled in bed. Gracie would be disappointed when she awoke on Christmas morning.

Instead of running to the tree filled with joy and anticipation, she'd... She'd what? Would they even make it out
of the swamp by then? Shae closed her eyes and prayed
for a Christmas miracle, prayed they'd all make it out of
this swamp alive, prayed for the strength to do whatever
was necessary to survive, because she didn't think she
had it in her to last another twenty-four hours slogging
through the marshes, scanning every direction, wondering where the next threat would come from.

And what about Mason? Clearly, he needed medical attention. He was injured, had to be physically and
mentally exhausted. And, with that, her thoughts had
come full circle. So much for the momentary distraction.
Mason. What was going through his head right now?
He couldn't have known about Gracie. However he'd
found out they were in trouble, she couldn't believe he
had anything but their best interest at heart.

But they were going to have to talk about all this. She
knew that...and dreaded it. Would he want to be a part
of Gracie's life now? As selfish as it might be, she'd had
Gracie all to herself for five years. Would she have to
share her with him now? What if he was with someone
else? Or even married? Would she have to share Gracie
with a stepmother and send her off for weekends and
holidays with people she barely knew, people who might
not watch her as closely as Shae did?

She sucked in a deep, shaky breath and blew it out
slowly. Okay, that wasn't fair. Mason had already risked
his life numerous times to save both her and Gracie in
just a few short hours. She might not know anything
about his life over the past six years, but she did know
he'd keep her safe.

And this was too much for her to contemplate now. But it was better than thinking about what was really gnawing at her—she would have to tell Gracie the truth, that Mason was her father. Gracie had never asked, so Shae had never brought it up. She figured if Gracie wanted to know, she'd ask, and Shae would have to decide how much or how little to tell her, depending on how old she was at the time. What would she tell her? That she'd been born from a night of passion with a man Shae had thought she'd loved and would spend the rest of her life with? Who'd then taken off and never returned? That she'd been an accident? No, she'd tell her the truth, that she was the most beautiful, incredible blessing God had ever bestowed upon Shae. And that she was loved more than anyone else in the world. If Mason could love her like that as well, then Shae would set aside her own paranoia and be happy Gracie had more people in her life that loved her.

Thankfully, movement in the shrubs to her right ripped her from contemplating the subject any further.

Mason emerged and swiped moss from his hair. "Okay, I found a spot, a downed tree with a thick canopy above it. I cleared space underneath where you should be able to lie low and hide until it starts to get light."

"What do you mean, *you*? Aren't you staying with us?" Shae massaged the bridge of her nose between her thumb and forefinger, easing some of the pressure the storms were causing on her sinuses. At least, she tried to convince herself that was the cause of the pounding headache.

"I have to backtrack, see if I can find where I lost my cell phone. It's in a waterproof case, so if I can find it, it should still work. If I can get ahold of Zac, he'll be able to track the phone and find us."

Shae didn't trust herself to speak; she was afraid she'd start blubbering at the thought of being left alone in the middle of a pitch-black swamp filled with critters, so she simply nodded. He was right. They needed help. "Do you think you can find your way back?"

"Yeah, I was careful to note landmarks." He slid a finger beneath her chin and lifted gently until her gaze met his. "I can find my way to the spot where we emerged from the water and then back to you. I promise. But it will be easier and safer for me to go alone. I won't leave you in the swamp, Shae. That's a promise."

She didn't say anything about the promises he'd made to her in the past, promises he hadn't been able to—or hadn't cared to—keep. Instead, she nodded and stepped back from his touch. "If you can't find your phone and you can make it back to the car and it's not entirely underwater, my phone is in one of the bags on the floor in the back seat."

"Got it." When he grinned, fire ignited in those electric-blue eyes, and six years disappeared.

She turned away. She had to. She'd trusted him once, with every ounce of her being, and he'd failed her, abandoned her.

"It'll be okay, Shae. We'll make it out of this."

"I know." She pulled Gracie closer. "But then what?"

His gaze slid to Gracie, and his smile faltered. "We'll figure it out. Okay?"

She nodded. What more could she do? He didn't know any more than she did about what would come next, except the obvious, that she'd have to go on the run again, might never be able to put enough distance between herself and the Kincaid organization to be safe. Best to just deal with the here and now and worry about the rest when the time came. She was a strong proponent of "put off till tomorrow what you can't fix today." She was also a strong proponent of taking time to pray, not only to ask for what she needed, but to meditate and listen for God's answer and to thank Him for keeping them safe so far. And that was what she'd do as soon as they were at the campsite—seek answers as to what path to follow.

Once she'd settled Gracie onto Mason's back once more, she followed him as he trudged even deeper into the swamp, scanning the ground and the surrounding area the best she could in the darkness, noting where the lake was in comparison to their position. While the sounds of nocturnal creatures would have made her uncomfortable, or more likely terrified her, it was more disconcerting to hear nothing as they hiked. Hopefully the silence meant the critters were holed up waiting out the storm and not that there were predators on the hunt—human or otherwise.

Mason stopped and gestured to a thick tree trunk that had long ago fallen and caught in the vee of the tree beside it.

Thick vegetation grew all around it, but a section had been pulled aside. The branches, leaves and other natural debris had been dragged out and scattered. A few more hours beneath the rain's assault and a passerby probably would not notice anything had been disturbed. It was possibly the perfect hiding place. "Did you make sure no other critters are in there hiding from the storm?"

"Absolutely." He lowered Gracie to the ground, then

slicked a hand back over his soaking-wet hair to stop the runoff from flowing into his face. The cut at his temple was still bleeding, though it seemed to have slowed.

Gracie pressed tightly against Shae, favoring her injured ankle, wrapped her arms around her waist and clung. She'd always been an independent child, curious and eager to explore the world—often to Shae's dismay. Now, Shae could only hope some of that curiosity and sense of adventure would return once this was over.

"Are you sure you're all right to go traipsing through the woods alone?" If he passed out, he'd probably be eaten by something, rain or not.

"I'll be fine." He moved closer and gripped her arms. "Promise me you'll stay put beneath the log until I get back."

She'd begun to shiver, and the two spots on her arms where his hands made contact were blessedly warm. She resisted the urge to hug Gracie even closer and curl into him. "I will."

He held her gaze a moment longer, then released her and shifted the shrubbery aside for them to enter the makeshift shelter.

Shae ducked beneath the log and into the small space. Claustrophobia assailed her immediately, and she had to fight the urge to flee back out into the open. While her vision had adjusted to the darkness outside, she had no hope of seeing anything in here. The odors of mold and rotting leaves and debris gagged her.

Gracie stuck close. She crawled inside, then sat next to Shae and seemed to relax against her. Perhaps the small, closed-in space brought her more comfort than fear.

Mason dropped to one knee and peeked his head in. "Okay?"

"We're good." But the thought of sending him out into the swamp to seek help for them didn't sit well. She pulled the gun from her waistband and held it out to him. "Take this."

He closed both hands over hers holding the weapon. "Keep it. You have to defend Gracie. If anything comes, make sure you don't hesitate."

Since she couldn't force words past the lump clogging her throat, she only nodded and hoped he understood. When he released her hand and backed out of the shelter, a chill raced through her. She told herself it came from sitting on the cold ground, soaked to the bone from the rain, and almost had herself convinced. Well, at least the shelter would block a good portion of the rain. She leaned back against a tree trunk.

"Mommy?" Gracie lay against her, tucked beneath her arm.

"Yeah, baby?"

"Who is he?"

Shae's breath caught, but she forced herself to exhale and braced herself for the coming conversation she was in no way ready to deal with. Mason had been so filled with faith when they'd met. He'd even guided her back after she'd turned away when doing the right thing had cost her so much. Then, while Shae had been pregnant, she'd found God and fully embraced His teachings, had raised Gracie with that same faith. In a way, her relationship with God had kept her feeling closer to Mason after he'd disappeared. But that didn't change the fact that her child's father had never known about her, had made Shae promises and then disappeared. "Mason is an...um...a policeman, who was once a...good friend."

She nodded and shifted to relax more comfortably against Shae, and a wave of relief poured through her when Gracie didn't ask any more questions. Cowardly or not, this was something she'd prefer to deal with after they were somewhere safe and dry and warm.

Gracie's breathing became more rhythmic, tension easing from her muscles as she dozed.

Shae let her head fall back against the tree trunk, praying for guidance. Her eyes began to drift closed, and she hovered somewhere between awareness of their surroundings and the welcome comfort of sleep. She hung there on that precipice, afraid to sleep, yet too exhausted to stay awake.

The sound of gunshots yanked her ruthlessly back to full alert.

Mason dived for cover behind a massive moss-covered oak tree.

Another shot rang out, and splinters flew from the tree on impact. He should have figured they'd wait on the bridge, probably with night-vision goggles. It made sense—it's what he'd have done. Why wander through a swamp when you could stake out the car and wait for them to emerge in the most logical place—the road where they'd entered the swamp?

He scanned the brush. Would they come in after him? Most likely. At least, if they knew it was a person hiding there and they hadn't just seen movement in the brush and randomly opened fire, hoping for the best. But what if it was an innocent bystander they'd just fired at?

He massaged his temples and admonished himself. The swamp was hardly filled with innocent civilians, wandering around in the pitch black during life-threatening thunderstorms. He could only hope it was the head injury clouding his judgment and not seeing Shae again… and Gracie. He had to get a grip, had to shake everything else off and concentrate on getting them to safety. Then, once he did get them somewhere safe, he still had a mission to accomplish, one he couldn't let go…for anyone.

He pulled his balaclava, now soaked and filthy, from his back pocket and wrung it out. Better to chance any bacteria that might be lingering than to have one of Kincaid's men see and recognize him. He was going back undercover after this was over. That was what he wanted, right? He pulled the balaclava on. He'd have to remember to remove it, though, before returning to Shae and Gracie. Shae would recognize him even with his face covered. Wouldn't she? But Gracie might be frightened.

Okay. So, now what? He hadn't been able to find his cell phone by the alligator's nest, so it was either lost in the water or still in the car, since he couldn't remember what he'd done with it after speaking to Zac. He never should have left the car without his weapon, but he'd been under fire, half-conscious and desperate to get Shae and Gracie to safety. Plus, Shae had a weapon, and he hadn't planned on splitting up.

Windswept rain beat at the trees and brush as a second storm unleashed its fury.

All right, there was no time for what-ifs. He needed a phone and he needed a weapon. The nearly submerged vehicle in front of him contained both.

If the curses amid the sounds of crashing through

brush were any indication, the men currently stalking him were no expert trackers, but they were still coming after him. Apparently, they hadn't all been content to wait on the bridge.

If he was quiet enough, he might just be able to outsmart them before Kincaid could send any more backup. Because whatever experts Sebastian Kincaid sent would slip through the swamp like the nocturnal predators they were. Thankfully, Mason only had to deal with those who had no experience in such matters right now.

That meant at least four—the two who'd been pursuing them, plus at least two more in the vehicle that had blockaded the bridge. He closed his eyes and listened past the sound of the rain, which would also provide him some cover when he decided to move. Two voices. He could definitely make out two different voices. That left at least two probably still playing sniper on the bridge.

The men moved closer, making enough noise to scare off every creature within a hundred miles. One of them fired a shot far to Mason's right.

He stood, pressed his back against the tree and prayed his plan would work, surprising himself that he'd reached so easily for the faith he'd lost. When the men were almost on him, both moving about a hundred yards to his left, he sucked in a breath and held it, then started to inch around the tree. Keeping his back tight against the trunk, he slid smoothly through the rain-soaked mud around the far side. Once they passed, he ducked into the shrubbery. There wasn't much time. He had to move before the attackers found Shae and Gracie. Their hiding spot wasn't as far into the swamp as he'd thought, his judgment probably thrown off by the detour to fight the gator.

He dropped flat on the ground and belly crawled toward the lake, then slid into the water as quietly as if he were a gator himself. Careful not to make the slightest sound, he moved through the dark water, keeping his head low.

Shae had already shut the headlights off, but he could make out the shape of the submerged car.

He paused when he reached the vehicle, laid a hand against the roof and took one moment to gather himself. He breathed in deeply through the fabric covering his face, then exhaled, once, twice. With the third inhale, he sucked in as much air as he could and went under. For just an instant, he opened his eyes, but there was nothing but blackness, so he squeezed them closed, pouring his full focus into his task. With his vision hindered, his other senses would have to suffice. He felt along the edge of the back window they'd escaped through.

There was no mistaking the muffled sounds of the gunshots, nor the sting of pain along his left biceps where a bullet struck. Another foot deeper and the density of the water would have rendered the bullet harmless.

Into the car? Or back to Shae and Gracie? He only had a split second to decide. Someone obviously knew he was there, and if they trapped him inside the car, Shae and Gracie would be on their own. And he'd promised her he'd return. Remaining submerged, he used both feet to push off against the car door and change direction. He dived deeper.

Where was the shooter? Not on the bridge. The car

was between him and them. They'd never have hit him. So, the shot had come from land. They must have been watching the car, maybe—probably—with night-vision goggles.

He propelled himself through the water as silently as any predator. He moved smoothly and pushed himself until he could no longer hold his breath, then pushed harder. When he couldn't stand another moment without air, when his lungs burned like fire in his chest and ached for release he didn't dare allow lest he leave a bubble trail for his stalkers to follow, he rolled over, let himself float toward the surface, until just his face emerged from the water, and exhaled slowly. He only allowed himself the briefest moment before inhaling and letting himself sink once again.

More than likely, his pursuers were searching near the car, expecting him to surface somewhere in the vicinity or continue to try to make it inside. It would be foolish to try.

He accepted the defeat. Making it into the car had been a long shot anyway, finding his weapon even less likely. He had, however, hoped to find Shae's phone, kept safe and dry inside her waterproof bag. They'd have to move to plan B.

Now, he needed to find a safe place to leave the cover the murky, black water provided so he could return to Shae and Gracie. Moving slowly, careful to avoid splashing and alerting anyone—human or otherwise—to his presence, he glided in their direction.

The fact that his pursuers had made such a foolish mistake, taking a shot without a clear target, gave him some hope they weren't Kincaid's best men. Had it been

Mason, he'd have waited for his prey to emerge from the vehicle or even make it back on land. Why risk a shot into dark water? Even if he'd come out of the car shooting, they'd have had the element of surprise. A sniper with night-vision goggles would have easily picked him off from the bridge.

The next time he surfaced, he risked lifting his head all the way out of the water. He had to get onto land before he became completely lost. He currently had no idea how far he'd traveled. Far enough he could no longer see the bridge, but that wouldn't take much, considering the weather. Surely he'd put enough distance between them that it should be safe. He angled toward the shore, keeping his head low. When no one had tried to put a bullet in him by the time he reached the marshy shoreline, he figured he was safe enough. Before he stood, though, he scanned a full circle around him, searching for any hint of movement or reflection that would indicate the presence of another.

When nothing moved, he crawled out of the water and straight into the thick vegetation lining the shore, then rolled onto his back and took a moment to orient himself, to breathe the thick, rancid air. He choked back a cough.

Clearly, there was no hope of escape or rescue tonight. With their pursuers staking out the car, and no idea which way might lead them to civilization and which way to certain death, they needed to find somewhere to hunker down. But not where he'd left Shae and Gracie. Even though the first storm had passed and the torrential downpour slowed, there was a lot more rain coming, and the entire area would flood quickly.

Zac already had his last known position, and Jameson Investigations boasted a wide network of resources, including trackers. Zac would come for them as soon as possible, and he'd deal with the men guarding the car. All Mason had to do was keep Shae and Gracie safe until then.

He turned over, lifted his head above the reeds and saw no one.

Then gunfire erupted in the distance. Only this time, a second round of shots followed on the heels of the first. Answering fire? Had Zac's people arrived to help?

As he debated whether to backtrack toward the bridge and check out the situation, a single gunshot pierced the night, followed by a sound that sent ice rushing through his veins. Despite how quickly it cut off, there was no mistaking the terror in the child's scream.

FOUR

Shivers tore through Shae as she held her hands out in front of her, trying to blink away the rain pouring down her face, impeding her vision. The gun weighed heavily against her back where she'd tucked it into her waistband so as not to further frighten Gracie. It didn't matter, though. She'd never reach it in time. Even if she'd been holding it in her hand, everything had happened too quickly for her to have used the weapon.

The gunman had come out of nowhere, crept up on them without Shae or Gracie hearing anything. One minute, she'd been sitting with Gracie, straining to hear past the pounding rain for any further gunshots that might indicate Mason was in trouble—or worse…which she couldn't even bear to think about—and the next, Gracie was gone, yanked out of the impromptu shelter before Shae could even react. She'd scrambled out after her, but she was too late to do anything but stand there trembling. She could only pray Mason had heard the warning shot the guy had fired, or Gracie's scream, before the gunman had slapped a hand over her mouth and cut it short. If he was even ali—

No. Don't even go there.

She didn't recognize the man holding Gracie against him, gun pressed to her temple, one hand covering her mouth. The fact that he hadn't donned a mask to cover his sharp features and short black hair wasn't lost on her. "P-please. Don't hurt her."

Gracie's tears tracked over his hand, mixing with the rain as she struggled to breathe through her nose, squirming as she clutched his wrist in both hands.

"I'll do whatever you want." Keeping her hands where he could see them, Shae rocked back and forth, inching slowly forward. Not that she had any hope of disarming him—she just needed to be closer to her daughter. "Please, let her go."

"Tell me who you're working with."

"What?"

"The identity of whoever tipped you off that we were coming after you." He squeezed Gracie's face tighter.

"I don't know what you're talking about." Her heart stuttered. "No one told me you were coming after me. I saw Kincaid's goons at Gracie's pageant and took off."

The gunman frowned and shook his head, clearly confused. Maybe Kincaid's henchmen didn't coordinate their attacks. "There has to be a mole in the organization. We got to Delarosa before she ever made contact with you. I'm sure of that. So, who's the rat?"

She started to squeeze her eyes closed, needing to think, but she couldn't tear her gaze from Gracie, who'd gone unnaturally still.

"My orders were to kill you and bring back proof you were eliminated, but it'll be even better if I can bring the name of whoever's betrayed Kincaid back to him. I'll move up to lieutenant for sure."

She had to stall, give herself time to find a way out of this, give Mason time to reach them. "What does Quentin want from me? Why can't he just leave me alone?"

"Quentin doesn't want anything now." A vicious grin split the man's face. "He's on his deathbed, barely clinging to life while his final arrangements are seen to, including who's getting promoted. And I fully expect to be on that list before the old man croaks. In prison. Where your testimony put him."

So many emotions warred for attention. While she should be relieved to hear the news about Quentin, guilt interfered. She'd been Quentin's personal assistant at one time, had liked working for the affable older gentleman. Had even considered him a friend. And he'd always been kind to her, treated her well, offered praise and bonuses when she went above and beyond. And then she'd found out exactly what he was. A mobster. A monster who planned to bomb an entire building full of innocent people just to eliminate a rival family. "So who do you work for, then?"

"His son. And Sebastian has vowed to avenge his father's death before assuming control of the family business."

An image formed, a scrawny teenager always lurking in the shadows at the office. But six years had passed, and a lot could change in that amount of time. She tucked the information away for later…if there was a later. Some part of her knew he was spilling too much information, sharing too much to have any intention of letting her leave the swamp alive. "Let my daughter go, and I'll tell you what you want to know."

"I'm willing to trade." He yanked Gracie tighter against

him, lifting her off the ground with the hand covering her face as she resumed her struggles. "*You* won't be walking out of this swamp, but I don't care about the girl. Tell me what I want to know and she'll live."

Shae struggled to think, tried to survey her surroundings in her peripheral vision without shifting her gaze from the gunman.

"Be smart about this."

Anyone who would take a child hostage would have no qualms about lying to get what he wanted. She didn't believe he'd let Gracie go. She was certainly old enough to repeat everything he'd just said to the police—thus implicating Sebastian Kincaid in Shae's murder—if he set her free.

The only thing holding her together right now was the fact that he didn't seem to know Mason was with them. He thought she'd been tipped off, that was all. Mason would already be on his way, would have started toward them the instant the man had fired his weapon. If he was still alive after the barrage of gunfire she'd heard before the gunman had taken Gracie. She shook the thought off, had to if she was going to survive this mess. Mason was fine. He'd been a trained FBI agent, had survived the past six years. And he would find his way to them. If she could stall long enough, or convince the gunman to let Gracie go, Gracie wouldn't have to find her own way out of the swamp, even if he did kill Shae. "Let my daughter go first. Let her run, and I'll tell you whatever you want to know."

She didn't shift her gaze from his, not even to look at Gracie, maybe especially so. The fear in her daughter's eyes might well send her over the edge.

"The name." He pressed the muzzle harder. "Now."

Gracie squeezed her eyes closed, starting to kick and flail harder.

"Please. I'm begging you. Just let her go, and I'll tell you." Shae made no attempt to hold back the tears or control the tremor in her voice. "She's a baby. If I don't give you the information you want, how hard could it be to catch her again?"

He studied Shae, seemed to contemplate the offer.

Movement in her peripheral vision snagged her attention. Mason? She didn't dare shift her eyes. Instead, she clung to the face of the man holding her daughter hostage. She memorized every feature. The scar running from the corner of his mouth to his right ear would make him easy to identify, as would the snake tattooed on the back of his gun hand. Of course, she'd have to live long enough to give a description.

Wind whipped the palms and brush into a frenzy, rain pelting them relentlessly. Marble-size chunks of hail battered everything.

"I'll ask once more. Who alerted you we were coming?"

"Please." She bit the name back, couldn't answer even if she'd wanted to, knowing Gracie would be killed the instant she said anything.

"I won't ask again."

Gracie yanked her head to the side, her screams muffled behind the man's hand. She kicked wildly and slid down an inch.

A man, dressed all in black, emerged from the woods directly behind the gunman. A black watchman's cap concealed his hair, black paint covered his face except for a salt-and-pepper goatee. He lifted a very scary-looking gun.

Shae lunged toward Gracie, reaching behind herself for the weapon tucked into her waistband. Shae might go down, but she'd do so fighting to give Gracie a chance to survive and get to Mason.

The gunman lost his grip on Gracie when she bit down hard on his gloved hand, and she tumbled to the ground, then scrambled through mud and puddles toward Shae. He lifted the gun, aimed directly at Shae...

"Run, Gracie!" Shae screamed and lurched toward her daughter as she whipped her gun toward the gunman. She'd never make it. *God, help me.*

Before she could get off a shot, he dropped like a rock.

The second gunman scooped Gracie up as he ran toward Shae, then shoved her into Shae's arms. "Run! Go! Now!"

Shae clutched Gracie against her, whirled and ran, crashing through the brush in a desperate bid for escape, plunging deeper into the swamp. Wind battered everything. Palm trees bowed in submission. And still, Shae ran blindly, blood roaring like a locomotive in her ears. The sound grew louder. The storm raged, unleashing its unrelenting fury. Hail assaulted her head, her face, her hands, stung her bare legs as she ran.

Then she slid, her foot going out from under her in the slick muck. She twisted, cradling Gracie's head, as she crashed to the ground amid a tangle of roots, landing hard on her hip. Pain ripped through her.

Without warning, a strong body tackled her from behind, tumbling her and Gracie over the roots and into a ditch alongside the massive tree and coming to a stop atop them both, pinning them to the ground beneath his weight.

Overhead the storm raged, the sound deafening. Trees snapped beneath its wrath, one after another in a steady path of destruction. Time stopped beneath the endless torrent. And then...

Quiet descended, but for the steady rhythm of the rain and their harsh, ragged breathing.

Shae sucked in deep lungfuls of thick, wet air.

"Are you okay?" The weight eased off her. Two strong hands gripped her arms and helped her to sit. And then Mason trapped her with his stare, those electric blue eyes delving deep as he searched for answers. "Are you hurt? Is Gracie hurt?"

He released her and lifted Gracie into her lap, pushed her soaked hair off her face, then pressed Mr. Cuddles into her arms. "I found him by the..." He hooked a thumb toward the gunman. "Over there."

The little girl hugged the rabbit close and buried her face in his muddy fur.

And Mason pulled them both against him, wrapping them in the safety of his embrace. Too bad it was only an illusion, as she'd learned all too well. "It's okay. You're okay."

"G-G-Gracie." Shae's teeth chattered as she tried to speak.

Her daughter sobbed, rocking a mud-covered Mr. Cuddles back and forth.

Shae had to get a grip, had to pull herself together long enough to make sure Gracie wasn't hurt. "Gracie, baby, it's okay. Shh..."

"We have to go, Shae." Mason stood and surveyed the area, then held out a hand.

She reached for the lifeline he offered, and he pulled her to her feet. A twinge of pain shot from her hip straight to her ankle, almost sending her back down again, but she braced herself against it, took a deep breath, held it, then blew it out, battling the pain. After two more breaths, her focus turned to the swamp. A path of destruction cleaved through the forest. For a moment, she thought it was from her flight from the gunman. "What happened?"

"A tornado, and it won't be the last."

"Tor…" The breath she'd struggled so hard for fled her lungs in a whoosh. Just what they needed—a tornado touching down as they tried to flee Boggy Meadows for good. But where would they go next? Shae had no idea. Certainly not back to New York. Somewhere else, then. Maybe a big city this time, where they could lose themselves in the anonymity.

"Come on, Shae. We have to get you somewhere safe, get Gracie medical attention for her ankle." He rubbed a circle on Gracie's back. "Sound good, Gracie? Are you ready to get out of here?"

She nodded against Shae without lifting her head.

"Right. Yes. You're right." He'd struck the exact chord necessary to get her moving again. She shifted Gracie until she could look into her eyes, ran her hands over every inch of her, searching for any sign of injury even as she spoke. "Gracie, honey, we have to go now. It's not safe here."

Gracie nodded, the expression in her eyes blank, then

laid her head back against Shae's shoulder with Mr. Cuddles between them. Her body went limp.

"Stay right with me." Mason took Shae's elbow, a pistol held out in front of him, and started to guide her back in the direction they'd come from.

Shae stopped. "We'll be walking right back into the gunmen if we go this way."

Gracie stiffened and whimpered.

He paused, looked back over his shoulder, eyes darting in every direction. "The man who killed Kincaid's gunman and told you to run. He's my boss, Zac Jameson... and he's a friend."

Shae frowned. "The man you called earlier?"

"Yes. He's waiting for us. He has the resources to keep both you and Gracie safe until we can figure out what's going on and decide who we can trust and plan a course of action." His hold on her arm tightened as he started forward again.

But she pulled away, took a step backward. "How can you be so sure you can trust him?"

"Shae, please. He has no involvement with the Kincaid organization."

She shook her head. "You can't know that."

"Yes. I can. There's no time to explain everything. Not now." He pushed the hair back off her face, cradled her cheek with his free hand and looked her dead in the eye.

The first stirring of the love she'd once felt for him struggled to surface but was instantly smothered by distrust. Maybe he sensed the chill, or maybe he was just in a hurry. Either way, he pulled back.

She refused to acknowledge her disappointment. Mostly.

. He guided her to a vehicle with an enclosed platform atop large treads instead of tires not far from where the gunman had held Gracie. The man with the salt-and-pepper goatee climbed out, exchanged a few words with Mason, offered a quick introduction to Shae, then disappeared back into the swamp. Mason helped her and Gracie inside, saying something about a safe house, then climbed into the driver's seat.

She watched the mysterious Zac Jameson retreat in the rearview mirror, issuing orders as he went. Mason was right about one thing—the man apparently had resources if he'd so quickly come up with a vehicle capable of moving through the swamp, as well as the team of agents currently hustling around the clearing. "You trust this guy?"

"Yes. Completely." He glanced in the rearview mirror then lurched forward.

"How can you?" Shae hadn't trusted anyone completely since…well… Mason.

"We can talk more about it later." He shifted his eyes toward Gracie, whose rhythmic breathing indicated she might have fallen asleep. Still, he was right. They couldn't be sure what she would overhear. "I can tell you that I had no choice but to leave when I did, Shae. Zac offered me the opportunity to go undercover in Kincaid's organization with the full resources of Jameson Investigations behind me, and I took it. I had to if I was going to keep you safe and get justice for Marty. Unfortunately, things didn't quite turn out that way."

"Why not?"

He hesitated, then offered a sad smile. "Let's get Gracie somewhere safe and settled first, then we'll talk more. But I will keep you safe, Shae. That I promise."

A promise he'd made before. And hadn't kept.

Mason glanced around the residential neighborhood as he held open the front door of the vacation home Zac had rented at the last minute—a center of operations they wouldn't be able to keep Shae and Gracie at for long—and ushered them inside. Although it would be acceptable as a temporary respite from the swamp, for the Jameson Investigations team to start a preliminary investigation while Mason, Shae and Gracie cleaned up and received medical attention, there was too much of a risk someone in the Kincaid organization would discover the last-minute rental—coincidentally attained at the exact time, in the exact area, where Shae had disappeared—and dispatch someone to look into it. No, as soon as the team doctor assessed them, they'd be back on the run. Mason would keep them on the move until Zac could procure a suitable safe house and get his team in place.

Zac's team would scout the quiet streets and secure the house. All Mason had to worry about for the moment was Shae's and Gracie's safety. Gracie… He was going to have to think about that situation at some point, but not now. He shoved the thought aside and guided them past the living room and dining room, where about a dozen agents operated in organized chaos as they set up the portable equipment they'd need to search for answers and coordinate a response, and down a hallway, then knocked on an open bedroom door. "Doc?"

"Come in, Mason." The elderly doctor had been part

of Zac's team from the beginning, a man Zac trusted from long experience, who'd saved the lives of more than one Jameson Investigations team member, including Zac himself, before he'd recruited him.

Dr. Rogers boasted a robust personality, kind blue eyes, a headful of thick, wavy white hair with a neatly trimmed beard and the ability to remain calm and see to his patients no matter the circumstances. Mason had seen him administer treatment amid a barrage of gunfire without blinking an eye. No doubt he could treat any physical injuries Gracie and Shae may have suffered, but he was also hoping he'd be able to help them cope with the trauma they'd faced in the swamp, since Zac would have already briefed him.

The doc offered a kind smile and patted a gurney that had been set up against a wall. "Why don't you put Gracie down here?"

Shae glanced at Mason. When he nodded, she inched into the room, surveying every inch of the place, including the blinds-covered window that would be their only escape route if anything went wrong.

Mason gripped the doorknob. "I'll be back in a little while."

Her gaze darted to him. "Where are you going?"

"Just into the other room to see if they've found a more permanent safe house and check if they've heard from the FBI or the marshals' service." Not that he blamed her, but the distrust and suspicion in her eyes stung. He dismissed the thought for now. Technically, the marshals' service had jurisdiction over Shae, since she was part of their witness protection program, but Mason had no intention of handing her over to them until he found out who had leaked her whereabouts. Because that was the only way Kincaid could have found her. Someone had talked. And he had every intention of making sure it didn't happen again. "Let the doctor check you and Gracie over, and then I'll be back."

He only paused for a moment to study Gracie. The little girl seemed strong and courageous, had certainly held her own in the swamp. When he'd reached the small clearing and found the gunman holding her, his heart had practically stopped. But his training had taken over, had allowed him to remove the threat posed by two other shooters concealed in the brush so Zac could go for Gracie. He already had so many reasons to be grateful to Zac, and now he had to add one more. He turned away, paused a moment in the doorway as the doc questioned Gracie about her stuffed bunny, then closed the door and walked away. There were more pressing matters at hand, even if some part of him screamed that he was nothing more than a coward.

He strode into the hustle and bustle of the command center and sought out Angela Ryan—a smart, handsome woman with sharp, angular features, rich umber skin and closely cropped black hair, who could light up a room with her thousand-watt smile. "Hey, Angela. What's going on?"

That smile was nowhere to be found when she turned her dark-as-night eyes on him. "We're still setting up, but from what we can tell, Sebastian Kincaid seems to have gone completely off the grid."

"You can't find him?" He took a monitor out of the box she'd just hauled in and set it on the desk.

"No. Nor anyone else from his inner circle." She went

to work unraveling and hooking up wires between devices at lightning speed.

"I recognized one of the men in the swamp. He was a midlevel soldier at best." Not that the man with the scar running down his face wasn't deadly—he was—but he didn't have the level of Sebastian's trust that would have earned him a spot at the grown-ups' table. Of course, Mason hadn't been able to reach that point, either. Even after so many years undercover in Kincaid's organization, he'd never made it past about the same level—his own fault, since he wasn't willing to do what would be necessary to move up. Scarface obviously had no such compunction. "Which means Kincaid is keeping his lieutenants close to home."

She nodded, lower lip caught between her teeth as she ran wires, rechecked connections and whirled the monitor around. "Which means he has something else planned—something bigger that he wants his best people for."

"That's what worries me." Somehow, they had to find out what Kincaid was up to. And Shae was probably his top priority if he was on a mission to prove to his father he was worthy of taking over the family business. He had to keep Shae safe, and his best chance was to stay undercover. "You're sure he can't find out Mace Lavalle is actually Mason Payne?"

"Positive." She paused to meet his gaze. "I set up your undercover identity myself, and I've monitored it since all this began. There is no connection between the two, and your cover has not been compromised."

He nodded. The last thing he needed was for Kincaid's men to figure out he was the mole. But, if Angela had done it herself, there would be no mistakes. And he needed to be absolutely certain of that, because… "You realize I'm going to go back in."

Angela stopped what she was doing, leaned against the table and folded her arms. "Have you discussed it with Zac yet?"

"Not yet."

"Mason…" She sighed. "Do you realize how fortunate you were to get out in time to protect Shae and Gracie the first time?"

"I know, Angela. Believe me." He raked a hand through his hair, searching for another solution, but he couldn't come up with one. The only way he could find out what was going on would be to infiltrate the Kincaid Organization again. As much as he hated to leave Shae and Gracie in anyone else's hands, eventually he'd have no choice.

"Do me a favor then?" She studied him, lifted a perfectly sculpted brow and waited.

"What's that?"

"Get Shae and her daughter set up at the safe house first. Give me a little time to get myself together here…" She gestured at the tangle of equipment half unpacked behind her. "Let me see what information I'm able to track down before I move to the new safe house. Besides, I sincerely doubt Zac is going to agree to you going dark under the current circumstances. And you know you have to go in with no contacts. Without being able to communicate with anyone, you'd probably just blow your cover worrying if Shae and Gracie are okay."

She was right. He couldn't risk contact with the outside world while undercover. Especially now that Sebastian had moved himself from underboss, having to do as his father ordered, to boss, with an agenda of his own. The man was nothing if not paranoid, often installing spies to monitor his own men. "We'll see."

She grunted, apparently satisfied that was all he could give her, and returned to her work. She glanced back up when he started to turn away. "And while you're at it, tough guy, go see Doc Rogers and get those wounds taken care of before you end up with an infection."

He grinned. "Yes, Mother."

She shot a rubber band at him and continued working.

Mason checked his watch as he strode down the hallway toward the bedroom the doc had commandeered as an examination room. He knocked and waited for a brusque "come in" before smiling to himself and pushing the door open. "How's it going in here, Doc?"

Dr. Rogers smiled at Gracie where she sat on the examination table while he worked on wrapping her ankle. He tapped the tip of her nose.

The fact that she smiled back at the kind, elderly man had at least a few of the knots in Mason's gut unraveling.

Shae smiled at Gracie from where she sat on a chair beside the gurney, concern etched in her too-taut features.

"Shae is all fixed up and ready for a shower, Gracie is just about done and going with her, and Mr. Cuddles is tucked in a pillowcase having his bath in the washing machine." Used to dealing with agents who didn't want to take the time to have their injuries tended, the doctor eyed Mason from head to toe. "So let's pretend we had the 'I'm fine,' 'No, you're not fine' argument, and I

won, which we both know I will, and you get your der-
rière on the examination table."

He winked at Gracie, patted her bandaged ankle gently
and lifted her off the gurney and into Shae's lap, where
the little girl curled up, her gaze, filled with curiosity,
riveted on Mason.

What could she be thinking? Was there any part of her
that recognized him as her father? Probably not, considering how young she was and what she'd been through
over the past few hours. Heaving an exaggerated sigh,
he took Gracie's place so the doctor could examine him.
The sooner he got this out of the way, the sooner he could
get Shae and Gracie to a more secure location. "Shae,
why don't you and Gracie go ahead and get cleaned up
now? I'd like to be on the road as soon as possible."

She nodded and stood. She was quieter now, or maybe
she just had nothing to say to him. Not that he could
blame her. No matter how much he'd loved her—and
he *had* loved her—he'd had no choice but to leave. He
could admit now, though, that he could have hung around
long enough to give her an explanation. If nothing else,
he could have said goodbye.

Did he still love her? Was he even capable of feeling
love anymore? He felt something for her, that he couldn't
deny. No matter how hard he tried to bury the feelings,
they insisted on clawing their way to the surface. Aside
from the sucker punch of emotions when he'd first laid
eyes on her, and the shock of recognition when he's spotted his daughter and recognized her... Huh. That was the
first time the thought of being a father hadn't brought
almost instant panic. As interesting as that was, it was
definitely a concept better left unexamined.

Angela was right. Maybe he had no business going back undercover. His thoughts were all over the place, a jumbled mess he seemed to have no hope of untangling. He couldn't even seem to get through answering his own question—was he still in love with Shae? His heart pounded painfully, his pulse rate skyrocketed and he shoved the question away. Maybe it was better left unanswered, since the outcome would be the same no matter what he decided. He would leave her again. He had no choice.

"There are shower supplies, towels and clean clothes for both of you in the back bedroom. Zac's men also retrieved your bags from the car and left them as well."

She nodded, thanked him and the doc, and started toward the door with Gracie in her arms.

"Oh, and they found your cell phone. One of the agents is going through it now, searching for any clue as to how Kincaid's men might have found you."

"You think I did something to—"

"No. Not at all. It's just standard procedure. People use their phones for everything nowadays, and you never know what might have tipped someone off."

She nodded, gaze averted. "What can I get it back?"

"You won't be able to have it back, but there's a new one with your things."

"What?" She paused. "No. I want *my* phone."

His gaze skittered to Gracie, then back to Shae as he willed her to understand. "It would be better not to take it with us, since it could be tracked."

"But… I know it's a small thing, but didn't have a chance to back up any of the pictures and videos of Gracie's pageant. It's our last normal memory." Tears shimmered in her eyes, tipped over her lashes. She squeezed her eyes closed. Of everything they'd been through since last night, the thought of losing her memories was what ended up reducing her to tears.

"Go ahead and get cleaned up and changed. I'll make sure they get all the pictures and videos off the phone for you before they destroy it. You can't sign in to any apps or access your cloud storage on the new phone until this situation is resolved, but we'll make sure you have whatever's on your phone now."

She blew out a breath and smoothed a hand over her daughter's tangled hair. "Thank you. I don't care about anything else. I just don't want to lose any of the pictures and videos of Gracie."

She didn't add since they'd most likely never be able to return there. She didn't have to. His heart, so hardened these past six years, threatened to shatter. "Why don't you and Gracie go ahead and get cleaned up? I'll find you as soon as the doc here patches me up."

She nodded, thanked the doctor again, then stood with Gracie in her arms and headed for the door.

"Shae?" He waited for her to turn back, then held her stare. "We need to talk."

Her shoulders slumped beneath whatever weight threatened to crush her, and she shifted her gaze. "I know."

FIVE

Exhausted and traumatized, Gracie had fallen asleep in Shae's arms as soon as they lay down on the twin-size bed. The scent of the baby shampoo that had been provided cocooned Shae in the illusion of normalcy as she stroked Gracie's still-damp hair. A soft knock on the door intruded on the only peace she'd found in the past twelve or so hours. As much as she wished she could remain frozen in that moment forever, she couldn't. She had to get up and face whatever the day might bring. So, filled with regret, she kissed Gracie's head, then shifted her onto the pillow and climbed out of the bed. Shae tucked Mr. Cuddles, whom one of Zac's female agents had brought in fresh from the dryer, into Gracie's arms, then lifted a blanket from the foot of the bed and laid it over them both. At least her daughter might be spared any more fear. For a few moments, anyway.

"Who is it?" Though she already knew, had sensed him lingering outside the door for the past few minutes, probably trying to decide whether to face the conversation they were about to have or flee to the easier task of hunting down a killer.

"It's me. Mason. Can I come in?"

With a deep breath for courage, she wiped her sweaty palms on the leggings Zac's team had left for her. While she appreciated all they'd done, and the man did seem to command an almost endless supply of resources, she still couldn't bring herself to trust these people as much as Mason seemed to. How could she? She'd trusted the marshals' service and the FBI implicitly during Quentin's trial, and they'd not only failed her, but at least one of them had betrayed them all. How could she help but view everyone with suspicion? And yet...

Everyone at Jameson Investigations had done so much for her and Gracie already, even at risk to their own lives. Seemed there were no easy answers, so she'd have to go with her gut, which said... What? The honest truth was, she had no idea. She'd trusted Mason with her life and her heart once, more than she'd ever trusted another person, more than she'd even trusted herself, and he'd let her down, walked away without a word. She sighed and opened the door. "Come on in."

His gaze darted instantly to Gracie, earning him a point or two in Shae's book, though he'd have to earn an awful lot more before he could even begin to gain her trust again. The fact that was willing to risk his life to protect Gracie might make him a good person, a courageous man, but she'd already known that about him. It was the choices he'd made that had caused the distance between them. "Can we talk?"

She glanced at Gracie, sleeping fitfully now that Shae had left her.

"The den across the hall has been set up as a conference room. If you leave both doors open, you'll be able to keep an eye on Gracie and hear her if she stirs." He stood in the doorway, waiting.

"Sure." If she didn't watch herself, his constant awareness of her concern for Gracie, and his obvious consideration for Gracie's safety at all times, might melt her hardened heart. As she nipped past him, the familiar woodsy scent of his aftershave brought back memories better left in the past.

She crossed the hall and entered a den with a sectional, a small desk in the corner and a round table with four chairs. Ignoring the couch, which begged for her to snuggle into a corner and pull a blanket over herself, Shae took a seat at the table. Best to keep her distance if she had any hope of escaping another broken heart. If not for Gracie, and the faith Shae had discovered over the past six years, she probably would never have managed to heal after the last time he'd left her. She'd believed him with all of her heart when he'd told her he'd enter witness protection with her, that they'd spend the rest of their lives together. When he'd disappeared, she'd gone crazy with worry. And grief. She'd never believed, not even for an instant, that he'd been the one to give up her location, the one who'd betrayed his own people and caused his partner to be killed. She couldn't believe that. But he *had* left without a word. And she'd worried for six incredibly long years that Kincaid had killed him as well.

She wouldn't go through that again. She couldn't. Clearly, she'd misjudged him, just like she'd misjudged Quentin Kincaid. If it was possible to be too trusting, Shae was. At least, she had been. Not anymore.

Seeming to understand her need for a buffer between them, Mason sat across from her—a huge concession, since she'd taken the seat with her back to the wall so she could see into the room across the hall where Gracie slept. The position Mason had always taken when she'd known him. She'd laughed then, hadn't understood the need to have a wall at your back so no one could sneak up on you, had never felt the constant need to look over her shoulder, hadn't comprehended what it meant to have your whole world turned upside down when you were blindsided.

He shifted the chair enough to see the doorway in his peripheral vision, despite the numerous agents currently working just down the hall.

A small smile tugged at her. She supposed some habits died hard.

"I don't know what to say to you." His gaze dropped to his hands, fingers interlaced in his lap. "The words *I'm sorry*—while I am, more than you could ever know—don't seem like enough."

"When I woke up the next morning and you were gone, no note, no goodbye, nothing, I didn't know what to think." There was no need to specify which morning she meant, since he'd fled after they'd spent only one night together. "Your partner had just been shot the night before, and I didn't know what to believe, whether to rage at you or grieve."

He swallowed hard. "I know, Shae, and I am so very sorry."

She fought back a sob, her emotions raw, as if she'd been dragged back six years in the past to relive the same pain all over again. "You already said that."

"Right." His eyes closed, and he nodded.

She sighed, struggled for control. That had come out harsher than intended, but the sense of betrayal, the grief at having not known whether he was alive or dead, the fear of raising the child that had been growing within her alone weighed too heavily for her to deal with. Except…

She hadn't been alone. God had stood by her, had led her to safety and protected her and her child, had given Shae time to heal and to grow stronger. Maybe it had all been because He knew she'd need to take a stand here and now, to get her life back so she and Gracie could stop running. But could she fight again? As she had against Quentin when she'd gone to the FBI, agreed to wear a wire and then testified against him? Did she have it in her to now go up against his son? And what about Gracie? If Shae stood her ground and fought back, Gracie would be in danger. No way could she let that happen. She would have to go back into witness protection. There was no other choice.

Confusion beat in time with the steady throb at her temples. She needed to deal with one crisis at a time. "You're forgiven, Mason. It's not about that. I forgave you a long time ago. I guess I just want to understand why. How could you have left without saying anything to me?"

He finally looked up at her then, a host of expressions warring across his features before finally settling on neutral, his mouth a firm, stubborn line.

Even if she had forgiven him, she still wanted…no, deserved some kind of answers—answers he didn't seem inclined to give. "You're the one who said we had to talk. So, talk. Or stop wasting my time and let me get back to my daughter."

He winced at that, massaged the bridge of his nose.

"You know what? The why doesn't even matter." When he lowered his hand, she searched his eyes for some hint of what he was feeling. "What I really need to know is, given the same circumstances, knowing what you now know, would you make the same choice?"

He blew out a breath, paused, then finally nodded once. "Most likely. Yes."

"Okay then." She slid her chair back, started to stand.

"Wait." Misery lined every feature. "Please, try to understand. I had no choice. I'll explain, just…just give me a minute. It's not easy for me to talk about all of this, and I'm sorry for that as well. I've been undercover in the Kincaid organization for the past six years. I have lived another life, the life of a criminal. I've done things I'm not proud of, things I wish I could go back and change, but I can't. I'm not a good person now, Shae. I'm not the man you remember."

She studied him for a moment while his gaze was averted, noted the pain and suffering and guilt that weighed so heavily. "I don't believe that."

When he finally met her gaze, a small flicker of hope flared in his eyes.

"Tell me. Tell me all of it."

After a quick glance over his shoulder out the doorway, he turned to face her more fully. "That last night I came to you, I came straight from the hospital."

"I remember. You'd gone to see Marty Bowers after he'd been shot."

"Yes." He raked a hand through his already-disheveled hair. "I was a mess. I needed you, needed to escape for a little while, forget about the reality of the situation for just that one moment. But I didn't use you, Shae. I loved you. At that time, I loved you with all my heart. We'd spent more than a year together while charges were brought against Kincaid and he was finally tried and convicted, and every fiber of my being ached to be with you, to marry you, to move on and spend the rest of my life with you. I wasn't supposed to fall in love with someone under my protection, but I did. I would have followed you into witness protection just to be with you."

She strained under the pressure of keeping her expression from betraying the hurt at his use of the past tense. Not that it mattered now, but it ached just the same.

"I didn't know then that I'd have to go undercover for years." He shrugged, lifted his hands, let them fall again. "Or maybe I did. I at least suspected it. But I was in denial. For the first time in my life I'd found happiness, and I couldn't bear the thought of giving that up—giving you up."

"And yet, you walked out sometime early that morning and never looked back."

"Yeah. And yet." He shoved the chair back and lurched to his feet so he could pace. "I received a phone call after you'd fallen asleep. Marty didn't make it. He died alone at the hospital, with no family members present, because it wasn't safe. Even though we had agents at the hospital, some posted outside his room, it didn't matter. Kincaid was too powerful, his reach too far. We couldn't guarantee the safety of Marty's wife and children, and we didn't know who to trust at the FBI, so Zac took them into hiding, which is what Marty would have wanted. But my partner died alone, and they never got the chance to say goodbye. And I hadn't stayed with him. I ran. Like a coward, because I couldn't face the fact that my partner was most likely going to die, couldn't deal with the certainty that the only way Marty could have been targeted was if someone had leaked his identity. And there were only a select few who knew."

"Is that why you went undercover?" Her heart ached for him. He'd been close with Marty, was godfather to his youngest child. "To figure out who had betrayed all of us?"

"Yeah. I had to know. First of all, to keep it from happening again so you would be safe. And secondly, to find justice for Marty." He stopped and faced her, hands propped on his hips as he finally made eye contact. "Plus, Zac Jameson came to me with an offer I couldn't refuse. By the time he reached out early that morning, he already had an undercover persona set up for me and was ready to get me into the Kincaid organization. Had I known that you were... Knowing about Gracie wouldn't have changed the circumstances. Most likely, it would have made me even more determined to go undercover and keep you safe."

Shae lowered her gaze to her hands, couldn't stand to see the pain in his eyes. She'd held on to her anger toward him for a long time. Maybe because it was easier to deal with than the hurt, the sense of betrayal, the fear, the grief. It wasn't that she didn't understand what he was telling her. She just needed time to process it all. For now, though... "Did you figure out who it was? The person who betrayed us all?"

He was already shaking his head. "I spent two years undercover trying to find out who it was."

"I thought you said you were under for six years?" Had he lied? Confused the timeline?

"I was." He dropped back onto his chair, as if finally sharing what had happened had left him weary. "I couldn't move up the ranks in the Kincaid organization enough to attain results. I couldn't…do the kinds of things that would have earned me a place as a trusted lieutenant. So my mission changed."

Well, she could certainly relate to that. She didn't know what to say to him. Not that she faulted him for the decisions he'd made; she didn't. But he could have talked to her, could have called and told her what was going on, could have left a note. Anything other than walk away without looking back. "You couldn't have gotten in touch with me? Not even once in six years? You couldn't have written a letter?"

"No, Shae. I couldn't break my cover. I didn't dare. You have to remember, you were at risk, too. With a leak in the FBI that I wasn't able to find and plug, there was always a chance someone would talk. Not to mention the possibility that Quentin or Sebastian had planted spies or surveillance equipment. I had to do a lot of things I regretted, even as I did them, and I couldn't take a chance my identity might be compromised—not for anything… or anyone. I'm sorry."

Shae ignored that, didn't want to know what he might have had to do to save her, to save Gracie. Did that make her a coward? What she did know, or was at least beginning to realize, was that he'd been just as alone as she had these past six years. He might not have gone into witness protection with her, but he'd still given up everything and everyone he'd held dear and assumed a new identity to go undercover to try to save her. He'd put himself at risk—

Everything in her went perfectly still as the scene in the swamp played out in her mind. She could still see the gun pressed to Gracie's head, still feel her own painfully rapid heartbeat, and she could replay every word the man had said to her. "Kincaid's men know there's a mole."

His eyes went as dark as the storm still raging outside, rattling the windows with its wrath. "What do you mean?"

"Did you hear any of what the guy in the swamp said to me?"

He shook his head, and a bit of a smirk played at the corner of his mouth. "I was kind of occupied."

"He wanted to know who tipped me off that they were coming."

Mason sat up straighter, scooted to the edge of his seat.

"He said he'd let Gracie go if I told him who had alerted me that they'd found me."

His leg bounced up and down, as it often did when he got jittery and ready to move on something, his mind racing so fast she could practically see the gears turning. No doubt, their conversation would be ending shortly.

"Can they figure out you were the one who infiltrated their organization?"

"No. There's no way." He yanked his phone out of his pocket, started to scroll. "Within hours of Marty's death, I had an entire new persona. I became Mace Lavalle, and Mason Payne ceased to exist until I returned to you."

He really had been in a kind of witness protection, just like her. "One more thing."

"What's that?" he answered, distracted as he scrolled and tapped.

"How *did* you find us?" Because only a handful of people would have been able to point him in the right direction, and one of them was dead. "How'd you even know we were in trouble?"

He looked up then, lowered his phone to his side.

"Maria Delarosa contacted Zac, told him she suspected your identity might have been compromised. The FBI had picked up one of Kincaid's midlevel enforcers. In return for a plea deal, he offered up the information that Quentin Kincaid was near death and that he'd sent Sebastian in search of you to prove his worth. An agent she was friendly with passed on the information—she didn't receive it through official channels. She said she didn't know who to trust, and she didn't want to call in case you were under surveillance. She was on her way to grab you from wherever you were and relocate you immediately. Zac sent an agent in to retrieve me. And before you ask, no, she didn't tell him about Gracie."

Shae simply nodded. What more was there to say? "So, what happens now?"

"Now, we have to figure out how Sebastian Kincaid uncovered your identity and where to find you." He pressed the phone against his ear. "Because you and Gracie will never be safe until we do."

Mason waited for Shae to return to Gracie. Then, with one lingering look at the two of them, he closed the bedroom door—as well as the door on the past—firmly behind him. He couldn't undo the last six years, and it would take a long, hard look at his choices to decide if he would even choose differently given the opportunity. A reflection he didn't have time for. He'd spent years beating himself up with guilt over leaving Shae without an explanation. He'd told himself keeping her safe by taking down the organization was worth it. But then what? If he'd accomplished his goal, would he have sought her out, returned to her, offered an explanation and begged for forgiveness? He had no clue, because every time that option had even flittered through his mind, he'd immediately shut it down. As he'd do again now.

He strode into the living room command center to find out if there were any new developments and access the new safe house information so they could get going. And stopped short when he discovered two of Zac's agents huddled in front of a monitor grinning widely as Gracie danced onscreen.

Until that moment, he'd only seen a frightened, timid child, a victim in need of protection, which he would willingly risk everything to provide. But in that instant, as Gracie wowed the audience at her Christmas pageant, not only with her dance moves but with a mischievous smile that had fire dancing in those blue eyes, some part of him shattered into a million pieces. Reality sucker punched him in the gut, robbing him of breath. This was the child, *his* child, whom he'd abandoned. A child so filled with life and love that it literally shone from her to encompass everyone around her.

"Hey, Mason." Angela gestured to the screen. "Get a load of Gracie. This kid's too much."

He simply nodded, unable to draw enough air to speak. He'd never thought of becoming a father, never had any desire to do so. And yet, knowing he'd missed five years of his daughter's life weighed heavily. *Oh, God, what have I done?*

Even if he hadn't known about Gracie, he had known Shae, had loved her. The night Marty had been shot, Mason had checked on him and then fled the hospital. Not from his injured partner or the circumstances or reality, but *to* Shae. He'd wanted nothing more than to reach her. He'd seen the stuffed bunny, sitting all alone in the gift shop window, and it had called to him, a kindred spirit perhaps. Because that was how Mason had felt—alone. And, for the first time in his life, frightened. What if he couldn't keep Shae safe? Marty was a well-trained, seasoned agent, and Kincaid had managed to get to him and leave him on death's doorstep. How could Shae ever hold her own against those people?

Would it have made a difference if he'd known she would soon carry their child? He'd walked away and betrayed Shae's trust, left her with nothing but a stuffed bunny she'd not only held on to but given to their daughter, so she would have some small piece of him. Tears threatened. He shoved them away.

They deserved better than him, deserved someone who wasn't as emotionally damaged as he'd become after so many years undercover, someone who hadn't spent so long living a lie, stealing, racketeering, collecting money for the very people who were trying to kill Shae and had succeeded in killing Marty. Which was not to say he hadn't orchestrated escape for many who owed Kincaid and couldn't pay—he had, with Zac's help. When he'd realized he wasn't going to move up high enough to find out who'd murdered Marty, since he wasn't willing to kill for the opportunity, he'd made it his mission to save as many as he could. He'd spent the majority of his time undercover smuggling out as many of Kincaid's potential victims as possible, sending them on the run with nothing more than a memorized contact number for Zac Jameson.

This trip down memory lane, while enlightening, served no purpose. After one last look at Gracie's incredible smile, he started to turn away, but his gaze caught on a guy standing on the side of the auditorium on the screen. "Wait. Pause that."

Angela shifted to business mode in less time than it took her to hit the pause button.

"Back it up." He leaned over her shoulder to study the screen as she rewound. "There. Stop it. Can you play it in slow motion?"

"Sure."

Onscreen, the drama played out at a much-reduced pace. Instead of focusing on Gracie this time, Mason watched the side door, held his breath until two men entered and looked around the room. One turned and walked out of camera range without showing his face, but she'd captured a good view of the other. "Pause it."

He tapped one of the men on the screen, a tall, beefy guy with a man bun and a goatee.

"You recognize him?" Angela swiveled her chair to a second keyboard along the ell made by the desk and a table and began tapping away.

"Yeah. He's one of Sebastian Kincaid's guys—an enforcer. Lucas Gianelli." He'd met Lucas before, had even worked with him once or twice. The thought of him coming after Shae and Gracie sent a shiver rocketing up his spine. "I didn't see him at the house or in the swamp, but he's a higher-up lieutenant, works directly for Sebastian." A plan was forming in his mind.

Angela's fingers flew over the keyboard as images of Lucas popped up on her monitor—a driver's license, mug shot, arrest record… "Do you think he's still alive? He could have been killed or captured in the swamp."

He was already nodding as he scanned the information almost as fast as Angela pulled it up. "Zac sent me pictures. I tried to ID the three guys who were killed and the one who was captured—and Gianelli wasn't among them."

"I'll let Zac know." She hit the speakerphone button even as she spoke and continued to enter commands one-handed.

"Find him, Angela." Because he was the key. If Mason found him now and was willing to work with him, gain his trust—while ensuring Shae escaped—he might be able to leapfrog up in the Kincaid ranks at last, without ever putting a bullet in an innocent person. Once his old man was gone and Sebastian assumed control, he'd begin his revenge tour and would be completely paranoid about letting any but his most trusted lackeys close to him. "Have you heard anything from Zac about the guy he turned over to the police until the FBI agents can get there to take custody?"

She left Zac a quick update via voice mail and hung up. "The guy's not talking, but Zac is still at the police station where he's being booked. Local law enforcement is cooperating."

"All right." Local police didn't always share information with private security companies, but Zac had resources he could tap when that was the case. One way or the other, he usually obtained the information he was searching for in time. Time they didn't have. "Is there a new safe house set up?"

"Yes." She waited for the printer to stop, then grabbed a stack of pages and handed it to him. "This is everything we could get on the men in the swamp, as well as the information on the safe house."

"Thanks, Angela."

She pulled a flash drive from her computer and handed it to him, along with a set of keys. "The drive contains the photos and videos from Shae's phone. The keys are to the dark gray SUV out front and the safe house listed on the last page there."

"Thanks again."

"Are you going to get some sleep before you leave?"

"No." He'd sleep better with a houseful of Zac's people to stand guard, but something was nagging at him, begging him to keep moving, and he'd learned to trust his instincts. "I'm going to wake Shae and Gracie now and get going."

"All right. Keep in touch, and I'll let you know as soon as I hear anything. Most of the agents will remain here to work for a little while longer, but I'm going to switch to the new safe house right away, so I'll see you there shortly." She hesitated as he turned to go. "And Mason?"

He paused and turned back. "Yeah."

"Zac had to notify the FBI and the marshals' service that we have their witness in our custody. They've agreed to share the knowledge with as few people as possible, but…" She shrugged and gave him a you-know-how-it-goes look.

Which he did. With a renewed sense of urgency, Mason knocked on Shae's door, then cracked it open when she called for him to come in. "We're leaving."

She stood from the armchair beside the bed and slid on new sneakers. Since the backpack Zac's men had retrieved from the car had been soaked, even though everything inside it had been protected, someone had transferred the contents into a new one, which Shae slung over her shoulder.

Mason approached the bed. "Will Gracie stay asleep if I pick her up?"

Shae smoothed their daughter's hair, kissed her temple. "She should. She was pretty exhausted."

"All right." He handed Shae the keys, then tucked the blanket around Gracie, picked her up and cradled her against his chest. "Let the agents waiting beside the door go out first, then follow them to the gray SUV in the driveway. Don't look around. Just keep your head down, go straight to the car and follow any instructions the agents give you instantly."

She nodded, lower lip caught between her teeth, terror filling her eyes.

He strode after her, stepping out into the rain and hunching over Gracie, trying to keep her dry as they hurried to the SUV. He made sure Shae got in as quickly as possible, then gently lowered Gracie to the booster seat and buckled her in, his gaze lingering for only a moment on the sleeping child he was charged with protecting, memorizing every feature to carry with him when he left her. Maybe Shae would give him a copy of the video from the pageant. He could always leave it with Zac or Angela for safekeeping, since he could never carry evidence of Gracie with him while Kincaid was in the picture. He climbed into the driver's seat, glanced around once more and made a right out of the driveway onto the narrow residential street.

Two of Zac's people followed in a black SUV and would accompany them to the safe house, where one would stand guard inside and one outside. The fewer people who knew their whereabouts, the safer Shae and Gracie would be. Of course, the FBI and marshals' service would eventually have to know where they were holed up. Hopefully, Zac would keep their exact location secret for as long as possible.

He crept through the quiet neighborhood, the *squeak, squeak, squeak* of the windshield wipers and the torrent of rain against the glass the only sounds. He glanced in the rearview mirror, slid a look at Gracie sleeping at an awkward angle in the seat, then looked over at Shae. "You doing okay?"

"Yeah." Shae stared out at the rain, tracing lines of water with her finger as they wiggled and squirmed along the window. "Just tired."

"Did you get any sleep at all?"

"No. You?"

"No, but I'm used to going without sleep. I'll still be okay for a while." If only there was something he could say to her that would ease some of her anxiety, lessen some of the tension coiled between them. Years ago, she'd have trusted him if he'd said everything would be okay. Now, she would recognize the attempt to alleviate her fear for what it was—a deception, even if well intended and even if he believed it at the time. "Why don't you close your eyes and try to sleep until we get to the safe house?"

She clutched the seat with a white-knuckled grip. "I left my entire life behind, sacrificed everyone and everything I knew in order to do the right thing and testify against Quentin Kincaid."

A man she'd worked more than five years for, whom she'd thought of as a kind businessman and friend. That must have been a betrayal, too, when she'd realized he wasn't a simple business owner but the leader of a major crime organization and a terrorist intent on wiping out an entire family to eliminate his competition and settle some personal grudge. When Shae had overheard a phone call from one of Kincaid's lieutenants regarding the assassination attempt, she'd dug deeper, terrified but determined to save lives. She'd presented the FBI with a plethora of evidence at great personal cost. Mason resisted the urge to reach out to her, try to soothe her. He doubted she'd appreciate the gesture, no matter how badly he wanted to ease her pain.

"Sometimes I wish I'd never overheard that conversation, never learned of his intent to eliminate the Pesci family," she said, so softly he had to strain to hear her over the rain pounding against the vehicle. "Does that make me a bad person?"

"No." He did reach for her then, gripped her hand in his and squeezed. "Absolutely not. It makes you human, Shae. You've lived in fear, not only for yourself but for Gracie, for more than six years. And you did it alone. That was a tremendous sacrifice. Does it make you a bad person for wishing it hadn't happened? No. But the fact that you came forward, testified under great threat to your own well-being and saved lives in the process makes you one of the most selfless, courageous people I know."

She squeezed his hand back, then released it to swipe away the tears tracking down her cheeks. "Thank you."

The loss of contact when he'd wanted so badly to reassure her hurt more than he'd admit to himself. But a glance in the rearview mirror at the black SUV with darkly tinted windows barreling up on the agents behind them had him shoving aside the sense of loss. "Hold on."

SIX

Instinct had Shae clutching the handle above the door as her gaze shot to the side-view mirror. "Is that Kincaid's men?"

"Most likely." He eased down on the gas pedal, increasing their speed, gaze flicking between the road ahead and the vehicle coming up fast behind them. He tapped the Bluetooth device in his ear and asked, "Did you call for backup?"

"On its way," the agent in the vehicle behind them responded smoothly over the car's speakers. "You go ahead. We'll run interference."

Mason accelerated just as the sound of gunfire erupted from behind them—not a pistol, but an automatic weapon of some sort. Shae turned to look over her shoulder, first at Gracie, who was mercifully sleeping through this, then out the rear window. A moment later, their bodyguards' vehicle lurched and rolled over twice before coming to a stop upside down. The SUV pursuing them didn't slow as it careened around the wreck.

"Mason." She gripped tighter, praying fervently for some way out of this.

"I saw." He made another call as the vehicle gained on them and relayed the situation to Zac.

Shae couldn't see any way out. On their right, an already flooded ditch cut off any hope of escape. To the left, a patch of woods separated the road from a set of railroad tracks, where a mile-long cargo train lumbered alongside them.

Mason accelerated. "Where can I get across?"

Across?

"Two miles ahead," came Zac's response through the earpiece.

He increased their already reckless speed. For an instant, the wheels lost their grip.

Shae clamped her teeth together hard to keep from crying out as they began to hydroplane and Mason fought the wheel for control. The last thing she wanted was to wake Gracie as another dangerous situation unfolded. Shae wanted to close her eyes, wanted to let go and trust Mason, trust God would see them safe, but she didn't dare. She couldn't.

Rain poured across the windshield faster than the wipers could keep up, reducing visibility to nothing more than a blur, and still Mason raced ahead.

"Mason…"

"It'll be okay. Just hold on."

Gracie's eyes opened, and she lurched upright, gripping the armrests on her seat. "Mommy?"

"It's okay, honey."

"Where are we going?" The little girl looked around, disoriented, clearly sensing some sort of danger but not seeming to comprehend where it was coming from.

"Somewhere safe," Mason blurted before Shae could say anything. "I'm taking you and your mom to a new house, where no bad guys will be able to find you."

She glanced at Shae for confirmation, and Shae nodded.

"Why are we going so fast?"

"So the bad guys won't know where we went."

Gracie nodded, seeming to accept Mason's answers, though she still clung tightly to the armrest with one hand and Mr. Cuddles with the other.

Mason began to pull ahead of the train.

Shae's heart jumped into her throat when she instantly realized what he'd meant by *across*. "Oh, no. No way. Mason."

"It'll be fine."

She stared at the train, literally thousands of tons of metal flying down the tracks. She'd often pointed them out to Gracie when they were driving alongside one or got caught at a crossing, and they'd try to guess what its variety of cars in all different shapes and sizes might hold. But the sheer size of that hulking beast speeding toward them… "But—"

"Can you do me a favor, Gracie?" Mason asked.

"Uh-huh."

"Just relax and close your eyes, okay, honey?"

"Why?"

He blew out a breath that under other circumstances Shae might have found amusing. Now, not so much. "It's a game."

Gracie gazed warily at him in the rearview mirror, an expression Shae suddenly realized was so similar to her father's. "What kind of game?"

"You close your eyes and take a guess how many cars you think are on that train, and your mom and I will count them and see if you're right."

She offered a tentative smile and closed her eyes, hugging Mr. Cuddles close. "Okay. They're closed."

He shifted in the seat, eased toward the shoulder. "All right, Gracie. How many do you think there are?"

As they rounded a curve, the tracks still running parallel, a dirt road came into view.

"Um. I think, like...a million."

Mason forced a strained laugh as he maintained a parallel course but pulled ahead of the roaring locomotive. "I bet you're about right. I'll count."

Shae held her breath, gaze riveted on the train, fear reaching up and choking her.

"One, two, three..." He swerved onto the muddy road at the last minute, probably taking the turn on two wheels. The long wail of the train's horn drowned out any other sound as Mason nipped across the tracks, crashing through the crossing gates, leaving them in splinters and barely making it ahead of the locomotive. Then he looked in his rearview mirror and muttered, "Please, don't try it."

The sound of the train's brakes screeching and metal being torn apart echoed through the deserted area.

Gracie screamed and clapped her hands over her ears.

Mason hissed as he let off the gas, finally slowing their forward momentum as they bounced and jostled down the dirt road that only seemed to lead farther into the endless expanse of forest. He tapped his earpiece. "We're clear."

"The vehicle in pursuit?" the agent asked.

"No. We're clear, but I need a way out of here since the train is stopping and I won't be able to go back that way." He kept his gaze on the mirror, and Shae wondered if the horror in his expression was reflected back at him.

"Why didn't they just stop?" Shae asked softly as she swallowed the lump in her throat and reached back for Gracie's hand.

"They were probably more afraid of returning to Sebastian empty-handed than they were of the train." He stopped the car and twisted to see the wreckage behind him, then used his sleeve to wipe the sweat from his brow, the only outward sign of stress he'd shown.

"What kind of monster is he?" Shae wondered out loud.

"You don't want to know." He glanced at Gracie. "You okay?"

She sniffed. "Uh-huh."

"Guess what?"

"Wh-what?"

"I think you were right." He smiled at her, then turned back around and started slowly forward. "I lost count, but it seems to me there were just about a million cars."

Her smile was tentative, but it touched her eyes. "That's what I thought."

His phone beeped with an incoming call, and he tapped his earpiece. "Payne."

"I'm worried the safe house might be compromised as well, but we've arranged for another."

Mason pulled his phone from his pocket and handed it to Shae. "Enter the address into the GPS, please. Go ahead whenever you're ready, Zac."

He gave her the address, and she programmed it in. Just about half an hour north of where they were.

"You can make a right onto the paved road at the next intersection. Just follow it around and it'll get you headed back in the right direction."

"Thanks, Zac. The agents behind us?"

"No."

He blew out a breath. His hand shook as he raked it through his hair, then pressed his fingers to his eyes. "Ah, man."

"Yeah. Let me know when you reach the safe house."

"Will do." And he disconnected, removed the Bluetooth from his ear and tossed it into the cup holder harder than necessary.

"I'm sorry about your guys." Any loss of life hit her hard, but she found it nearly unbearable that she couldn't help feeling some sense of responsibility for all of these deaths. She closed her eyes, prayed for the souls of all those who'd died protecting them, prayed God would have mercy on those who'd died pursuing them, even if they had meant to harm or kill them. She wondered what could have gone so wrong in their lives that could have turned them into killers. Or had they simply been born evil? She had a feeling there was nothing simple about any of this.

They rode in silence, the hum of the tires against the pavement lulling Gracie back to sleep. The rain had finally eased up the farther north they'd driven and was now nothing more than a steady drizzle. Shae's mind begged her to allow it to shut down, even if only for a few minutes. She needed rest, had to have some downtime to recharge. Her eyes drifted closed, and before she knew it, she was back in the swamp, Gracie held tightly against the gunman, weapon pressed against—

She jerked back awake with a gasp.

"It'll take a while." Mason's eyes held only understanding.

"I suppose." Though she doubted she'd ever be able to close her eyes again without reliving that terror. "I just hope Gracie will be okay when this is all said and done."

"Zac has counselors on his team as well." He shrugged

and turned his attention back to the road. "It might be something to think about."

She nodded her appreciation. "Thank you."

"If you decide that's the route you want to go, let me know and I'll talk to Zac."

She tilted her head, studied him. "That's it?"

"What do you mean?"

"You don't have an opinion? Don't want to discuss it? You're just going to leave it up to me to decide what's best for Gracie?" As if it didn't matter to him one way or the other?

He frowned. "Why wouldn't I?"

She shook her head. "Nothing. Forget it."

He started to speak, then seemed to think better of it and let the subject drop as the computerized voice of the GPS led him through a small town that appeared as if it had been suspended somewhere in the mid-1900s.

She couldn't decide whether she should be angry or relieved that he'd leave such an important decision completely up to her. Maybe he just figured she knew what was best for Gracie, since she had the benefit of five years raising her. Or perhaps he just wasn't interested in playing a role in her life. Either way, it shouldn't bother her. She'd always raised Gracie on her own and was perfectly capable of making decisions based on what would be best for her daughter. Had even dreaded the idea of sharing her when Mason first reappeared. So what was her problem? Why did it matter that Mason didn't even want to discuss Gracie's needs?

The answer hit her like a battering ram—because he wouldn't be there to discuss anything. He was going to get them somewhere safe and then leave. Again. Which was fine, especially since it wasn't only her heart on the line this time. She'd loved him once—probably still did, if she were being honest with herself—but she wasn't alone now. If he became a part of their lives and then took off again, Gracie would be hurt, too. No one needed that. The best thing they could do was work together to put an end to the Kincaid organization and allow Shae and Gracie to move on with their lives in peace. Who knew? If things went right, maybe they could even return to Boggy Meadows and resume the life they'd just been forced to abandon. Did she dare hope for that, or was it a fool's dream? Either way, whatever the future held, it seemed it would be her and Gracie on their own navigating it. A happily-ever-after with Mason Payne wasn't meant to be.

"Mommy?"

She ignored the hole in her gut. "Yes, baby?"

"Is it almost time to go to Katie's Christmas Eve party?"

Even knowing it wasn't a possibility, Shae glanced at the dashboard clock and couldn't believe it had been only around fourteen hours since their ordeal had started. "No, sweetheart."

"But we're supposed to help set up," Gracie whined.

"I know, baby, but it's not safe to go back to Boggy Meadows right now."

"Because of the bad men?" Soft sniffles had Shae digging through the backpack for tissues.

She handed a small package back to Gracie and kept one for herself. "Yes."

"But, Mommy, I really want to go. How about church in the middle of the night?"

Midnight mass on Christmas Eve had been a tradition since before Gracie was born, where Shae would often pray for Mason's safety and that he'd return to them. She could only laugh at the irony. This mess wasn't exactly what she'd had in mind. "We'll have to see."

Gracie kicked the back of Shae's seat, startling her. "It's not fair. You promised we could go."

"I know, honey, but there's nothing I can do about this situation. It's beyond my control, so how about we just make the best of it?" She sucked in a deep breath, searching for patience. None of this was Gracie's fault. She wasn't even old enough to understand most of what was happening.

Gracie gave up arguing and started to cry instead. Shae preferred the anger. With a sigh, she turned to look Gracie in the eye over the seatback. "Listen to me, Gracie. I promise you, once this is over, we'll have a Christmas Eve party, okay?"

She sniffed and scrubbed her hands over cheeks that were red and raw from crying. "A party at our house?"

Something Shae had never done before. While they often attended church functions or gatherings at Reva's house, Shae only rarely entertained. And when she did, it was limited to Reva and Katie. Under the circumstances, she'd never been comfortable inviting a group of people into her home, her safe space. Except now it was no longer safe. Could she ever return to that little house? Even if they did take down the Kincaids? She doubted it. "Yes, honey. We'll have a party at our house, and you can invite Katie and Miss Reva and some of your friends from school and faith formation if you want."

"Uh-huh. Okay." As she scooted up straighter in the seat, the package of tissues dropped unnoticed from her lap to the floor. "And can we have pizza and soda…"

Gracie got herself all wound up with plans for a party that would probably never happen as Mason spoke to Zac on the phone, off speaker now. Shae's thoughts turned inward, to what they'd have to do if she ever hoped to have the life she'd just outlined for Gracie. She'd always been content to stay at home with Gracie, but now she wanted more than that. She wanted to live her life to the fullest, not just survive. And in order to do that, Sebastian Kincaid had to be found and dealt with. She'd gotten through one Kincaid trial—barely—and she'd get through this one, too. Which meant getting enough evidence to put him away for good.

She saw no other choice. Mason would have to leave them to go undercover.

Mason backed into the driveway of a small stucco house on the outskirts of town. Situated in one of thousands of neighborhoods just like it that could be found across Florida, nothing about it stood out. Perfect for their needs. "Wait here."

Leaving Shae and Gracie in the running SUV in case they had to make a quick getaway, Mason climbed out and surveilled the neighborhood. He walked the perimeter of the house, separated from the houses on either side by about thirty feet and a low, tan stucco wall. Satisfied that everything seemed quiet, Mason punched the key code into a lockbox on the front porch, took out the key and opened the front door. A quick recon of the minimally furnished three-bedroom, two-bathroom house showed all was well.

Leaving the front door standing open, he jogged back

to the SUV and opened the passenger-side door. "You get Gracie. I'll get the bags."

Shae nodded without saying anything. She'd been quiet since Gracie's tantrum, and Mason hadn't known how to ease any of their fears. They were right to be afraid.

Without a word, he waited at Shae's side, trying to appear casual as he slowly scanned the oak-lined street, the yards, the few people walking along the sidewalks—one guy chasing after a kid on a tricycle, a woman walking a golden retriever and an elderly couple in what looked like brand-new jogging suits speed walking like their lives depended on it.

To anyone who happened to notice, Mason, Shae and Gracie would look like a family who'd rented an Airbnb for the holidays. As soon as Shae had lifted Gracie out of the car and into her arms, Mason closed the car door behind them and hurried them inside. There would be no lingering in the yard, no strolling the sidewalks, no recording Gracie's antics. Because they weren't a family. Shae and Gracie were a family, and Mason was their bodyguard. He'd do well to remember that lest he become too attached, just like the first time he'd been charged with Shae's protection.

He stuffed the keys into his pocket and set Shae's backpack on the tiled foyer floor beside the door. "There are two bedrooms next to each other in the back of the house—one with a queen-size bed and one with bunk beds—you can take either or both. The one closest to the living room will be for the FBI agents they're send—"

"Whoa. Wait. What?" Shae froze with Gracie half lowered to the floor for a moment before straightening, her daughter still in her arms. "What FBI agents? I thought you were protecting us."

"I am." There was no need to elaborate on the fact that he was no happier about the situation than she was. It would serve no purpose but to worry her even more. "I'll sleep on the couch now and then when I need to, but the FBI agents will be here, too. Whether we like it or not, they're still in charge of the official investigation into the Kincaids."

She hugged Gracie closer, eyed the front door over her shoulder, looking about ready to turn and bolt.

"Zac will have his own people in place as well, but the FBI presence is nonnegotiable." And Zac had negotiated, insistently…and loudly. At least he'd managed to talk them down from sending marshals as well. The marshals' service would only take over if and when Shae had to go back into official witness protection. "They wouldn't budge on it, Shae, so Zac had no choice but to acquiesce if he wants them to share information. It makes more sense to cooperate and share information than to run two separate investigations."

"You'll still be here, though?"

He wouldn't lie to her, nor would he flee in the night like a coward, but he didn't want her to be any more frightened than necessary, either, so he offered her the best he could. "Until I know you're safe."

She said nothing, simply stared at him with Gracie clinging tightly to her neck, legs wrapped around Shae's waist like she might never feel safe enough to let go again.

"Look, Shae." It would be a lot easier to convince her this was necessary if he was fully onboard himself. But, while he understood the importance of interagency cooperation, appreciated the willingness of local authorities to coordinate with Zac's team, he still didn't like the idea of anyone he didn't know involved. Not when they hadn't plugged the leak after last time. "The agents they're sending were handpicked by the local field office director. They have no connection to anyone in the Kincaid organization, but I'm told they all have a background in dealing with organized crime. It's the best-case scenario under the circumstances."

The doorbell rang, and Shae and Gracie both whirled toward the sound.

Whoever was out there could wait a minute, because he refused to force her to accept any situation she was uncomfortable with. If she wouldn't agree to the FBI agents Zac had only told him about on the drive here, they'd have to figure out something else. "If we go on the run, just the three of us, it would keep me from having any active role in the investigation, which could prolong this."

"How do you plan to prove Sebastian Kincaid is trying to ki…uh…" She looked down at Gracie, rubbed circles on her back. "Even with my testimony about what the guy in the swamp said to me, it's still not evidence. How can you prove he's involved?"

"I don't know yet, but we're going to. And, hopefully, take down his entire organization with him."

"Seriously?" She lifted a brow. "We couldn't dismantle the Kincaid organization when we put their boss in prison. What makes you think you can do so now?"

"Because until now, despite being in prison, Quentin was still in charge. Sebastian Kincaid lacks his father's business sense, his discipline and his discretion.

It's no surprise his father is testing him. He'll mess up, and when he does, we'll grab him."

The doorbell chimed again. This time, Shae nodded, and he opened the door to two people dressed in dark suits that screamed federal agents: a woman with soft features and blonde hair pulled back into a ponytail and a tall man with black hair going gray at the temples. One look at the equally easily identifiable sedan parked at the curb had Mason biting back a sigh.

The woman held out her hand. "I'm Agent Cassidy Monroe, and this is my partner Agent Jimmy Ronaldo."

Once introductions were made, Cassidy held up a large fast food bag and tipped it back and forth. "Who's hungry?"

Gracie glanced at Shae, who nodded. "Me."

"Do you like chicken nuggets?"

Gracie nodded, seemingly shy with the new agents. It stung that Mason had no clue if it was normal for her to be leery of strangers or if that was a new development since being attacked.

"Why don't you and I go into the kitchen and set up lunch while your mom talks to Mason and Jimmy for a few minutes? You'll be able to see your mom from the table." Cassidy leaned over conspiratorially. "And I'm pretty sure there are some chocolate chip cookies in this bag, too."

Gracie grinned and wiggled out of her mother's arms. When Cassidy reached out to take her hand, Gracie cringed away, then turned back to look at Shae twice in the short walk to the kitchen.

As soon as they were out of earshot, Jimmy updated them on the progress so far. "I don't know how much you've been told, but the three men who were killed in the swamp have all been identified, and they're all connected to the Kincaid organization. The one who survived was taken into custody and refused to answer questions without an attorney present. Since the attorney of record is on Kincaid's payroll, we have little to no hope he'll take a plea deal in return for testimony against Kincaid."

"I'm not surprised." Sebastian liked control—it kept things running his way. The attorney would no doubt report right back to him if their suspect talked, and the guy would have an accident soon after, long before he ever had a chance to testify.

That was one of the biggest reasons law enforcement could never get to Kincaid—witnesses, or lack thereof. The few who had ever been willing to talk were killed or made to disappear before they saw a courtroom. Shae was the rare exception, someone who'd stumbled onto information accidentally and had managed to get to law enforcement and be placed in protective custody before Quentin Kincaid had even realized what was happening. Because he'd not only trusted her but had underestimated her as well. And even though they'd gotten Shae to a safe house early on, it hadn't stopped Kincaid from finding her. They'd had to move her several times that year and had never found the leak. "What about Lucas Gianelli? The guy I identified from the video at Gracie's pageant. Were you able to locate him or determine the identity of his partner?"

Jimmy shook his head. "No, nothing."

These people were like shadows, hovering, then disappearing in an instant. Frustrated, Mason tried to think.

"We did, however, locate Sebastian Kincaid."

That must have just happened, since Zac hadn't informed Mason yet. "Where is he?"

"He landed in a private aircraft at a small field in central Florida sometime yesterday morning."

So he'd come to Florida to oversee the situation himself. Not surprising, considering what was at stake. "Where is he now?"

Color peaked in the agent's cheeks. "We don't know that, just that he arrived in the state. We have people working alongside Zac Jameson and local police to track his movements from the time he landed."

Mason only nodded. The fact that they'd been able to place him in Florida at all was an accomplishment. "All right. Thank you."

"Sure thing." He hesitated, his gaze flitting to Shae.

"It's okay. Speak freely." Mason had no doubt Shae would handle whatever information the agent shared, just like she'd handled everything else that had been thrown at her so far, throughout the trial and during her life afterward, including the past twenty or so hours.

He winced. "They found the leak in the marshals' office."

Rage poured through Mason. He'd known there must be a leak, but having it confirmed fueled the anger he'd suppressed. "And?"

"He's dead, killed in an 'accident'..." Jimmy rolled his eyes. "A few days after Maria Delarosa was killed."

"Before Sebastian arrived."

"Yeah. Assumption is, Sebastian waited until they'd located Shae, then had the agent eliminated and made the trip." *To see to things personally*, no one said out loud. "That's why no one answered the phone when Shae tried the emergency contact number. The mole took care of that."

"That makes sense." Attack Shae while the marshals' service was scrambling to get things in order. "They had to know someone was dirty."

"It would have taken a little time to figure out who they could trust in the position."

No one. That was the simple answer. Because, some-how, it seemed Sebastian Kincaid had a way of getting to whomever he needed, if not through bribery or black-mail, then with intimidation. Or had it been Quentin who'd overseen the operation? "Yeah."

"So, that's it for now. I'll update you as soon as I know anything else. We've been ordered to give your boss full cooperation. That man definitely has some pull."

Mason grinned. *Pull* was a nice word for it. "That he does."

Jimmy shook Mason's hand, nodded to Shae, then joined his partner in the kitchen.

Shifting so he and Shae could both keep an eye on Gra-cie, who was chatting happily with Cassidy while munch-ing on chicken nuggets and fries, Mason tried to order his thoughts. "I'm going to step outside to make a few calls. I want to confirm everything Jimmy told us with Zac."

She frowned. "You don't trust him?"

He glanced into the kitchen, where the two agents sat talking quietly. "It's not that I don't trust him specifi-cally. I don't trust anyone."

"I can understand that." She caught her bottom lip be-tween her teeth, hesitated only a moment. "But you do trust Zac?"

"Completely. Kincaid has a way of getting to people—

he bribes them, threatens them, whatever it takes to gain cooperation—but he can't get to Zac." Of that Mason was absolutely certain.

Shae frowned, understandably leery of everyone. "How can you be so sure of that?"

"Because Marty Bowers was Zac's stepbrother."

Shae gasped.

"Yeah." And when he'd gotten the opportunity to send Mason undercover, he'd jumped at it. "He never forgave himself for not being at the hospital when Marty died, even if he had been protecting his family."

"That's awful."

"Yes. It is. That's why I trust Zac so completely. Not only is he a close friend, but he would never help any member of the Kincaid organization for any reason. You don't spend six years trying to take someone down only to turn around and join them."

"No." She checked Gracie again then lowered her gaze. "No, I suppose not."

Mason reached out, used one finger to lift her chin until she met his gaze. "I'm not going anywhere until you're safe. I'm going to step outside to make some calls right now, but if you need me, just call my cell phone. The number is programmed into your new phone." She held his gaze, then nodded. "Lock the door behind me and go have something to eat with Gracie. Do not open the door for any reason. Zac's people will be here soon, but the FBI agents will open the door for them if I'm not back in yet."

She nodded again.

He opened the door and walked out, determined to find answers.

SEVEN

Gracie shook Shae's shoulder, yanking her from sleep. "Wake up, Mommy. It's Christmas."

She pulled Gracie into her arms and hugged her tight, then kissed the top of her head. "Merry Christmas, baby girl."

Gracie flipped onto her stomach in the queen-size bed they'd shared, leaving the bunk beds for Mason or any of the other agents who might need to sleep. She propped her elbows on the pillow and rested her chin in her hands, her eyes filled with hope. "Do you think Santa Claus found me here?"

"Oh, Gracie." They'd gone to bed early the night before with no Christmas Eve celebration, since all of the agents were working; no mass to attend, since Mason had said there was no way to protect them in a public setting; and no further information on a permanent placement for them. She'd thought Florida would be far enough away from New York for them to be safe, and she'd been wrong. It seemed maybe nowhere would be far enough from the Kincaids. And now, she was going to have to disappoint Gracie once more. "Honey, I think maybe—"

A knock at the door interrupted, buying her a precious

moment or two before having to watch the joy drain out of her child once again.

"Who is it?"

The door opened a crack, and Cassidy poked her head in. "I thought I heard a little girl awake in here. Merry Christmas."

Gracie sat up and bounced on the bed. "Merry Christmas."

She looked over her shoulder then back at Gracie, grinned and hooked a thumb down the hallway. "I think there might be a surprise out here for you. If you're ready to get up…"

Gracie launched herself off the bed so fast Shae had to laugh. "Did Santa come?"

Cassidy winked at Shae. "I do believe he did."

Gracie's excited squeal almost brought Shae to tears. It sounded like Jameson Investigations provided everything, not only what they needed to keep them safe but even gifts for Gracie.

"Why don't you and your mom get dressed and come on out into the living room? Breakfast is just about ready, too."

"Can we, Mommy?" She clasped her hands together. "Please."

"Sure thing." They dressed quickly, Shae donning leggings and a sweatshirt from her flight bag and Gracie putting on her leggings and T-shirt from the day before, since most of what was in the bag didn't fit, including the too-small pajamas she'd worn to bed.

Gracie kept up a nonstop stream of chatter, excited about the possibility of gifts, wondering what they'd have for breakfast, asking if they could maybe have something special for dinner. As excited as Shae was to see some life return to her daughter's eyes and color to her cheeks, she had no idea what to expect when they walked out. No one had said anything to her before she'd gone to bed.

Shae laid a hand on the doorknob, turned to Gracie and smiled. "You ready?"

"Yup." She gripped Shae's hand, hers feeling so delicate, so fragile.

The fact that anyone could want to hurt this child sent a surge of anger rushing through her. She tamped it right back down. No way would she let them take this moment with Gracie from her. "Don't forget to use your manners."

"I know, I know." She bounced up and down, swinging Shae's arm. "Come on."

Shae laughed and swung the door open, and the scent of bacon frying hit her full force. Her stomach growled, and she clapped her free hand over it.

The fact that Gracie stayed beside her, her grip tight as they walked down the hallway, instead of bounding ahead told her the wounds from yesterday's trauma may have diminished, but they were far from gone. She'd have to consider Mason's suggestion and ask him about counselors later.

Shae stepped into the living room and stopped short. Her mouth fell open.

Gracie squealed again, then bolted across the room to the Christmas tree in the corner.

Cassidy nudged Shae's ribs with an elbow. "She seems happy."

"I don't understand." A small tree had been set up in

the corner, draped with about a thousand multicolored lights reflecting from red, green and gold glass balls. A pile of gifts was spread beneath the tree. She closed her eyes, shook her head, opened them again. Nope, not a hallucination brought on by too much stress. It was all still there.

Then Cassidy leaned closer and whispered, "Mason didn't want her to go without getting to celebrate Christmas."

"I…" But she had no clue what to say, couldn't have forced words past the lump in her throat if she'd tried. How could he have gotten all this done so quickly? The fact that he'd even thought to do it at all filled her with warmth. She glanced into the kitchen, where three agents sat at the table and two were busy setting out platters of food. "Where is Mason?"

"He had to run out, but he'll be back any minute." She waggled her eyebrows. Wherever Mason had gone, Cassidy was obviously in on it—and highly amused.

Gracie picked up a gift from under the tree, held it close to her ear and shook it gently back and forth. "Mommy, this one's for me. It's from Santa Claus. See? I knew he would find me. Can I open it?"

"Actually," Cassidy intervened, as she checked something on her phone, then stuffed it quickly back into her pocket, "why don't you hold off for a minute?"

Shae's gut cramped. The last thing she wanted was to pull Gracie out of there and go on the run again. *Oh, please, not today. Please give us just one day to rest, to recuperate, to celebrate.*

"Okay." Gracie set the package down, ran back to Shae and threw her arms around Shae's legs.

Cassidy bent low to talk to her. "Can you do something for me?"

Gracie looked at Shae, then back at Cassidy. "Okay."

She smiled. "Close your eyes."

Gracie did as instructed.

"Keep them closed, now." She walked to the front door, checked that Gracie still had her eyes closed. "No peeking."

"I won't."

Shae was happy to see Gracie seemed to be coming out of her shell a little and thrilled she'd remembered to use her manners.

Then Cassidy swung the front door open, and Mason plunged through, a wiggling mass of golden fur on a leash at his side. He met Shae's gaze as Cassidy first shut the door behind him then discreetly disappeared into the kitchen. The look he gave her—half triumph, half apology, mostly am-I-in-trouble—nearly made Shae laugh out loud. She gave him a nod.

Then his expression turned to pure joy. "You can open your eyes now, Gracie. We have a special visitor."

He led the dog toward her as Gracie's eyes popped open.

She screeched loud enough to shatter every eardrum within half a mile. "A doggie!"

The little girl dropped to her knees and wrapped her arms around the ball of fur. The dog licked her face, and she laughed out loud. "He's so cute. What's his name?"

"Storm."

"Is he your dog?"

"Actually, he's a police dog." He reached out, ruffled her dark hair. "We don't get to keep him forever, but he will stay with you and help keep you safe until we find the bad men."

Gracie lowered her face into the dog's fur and sobbed.

Mason looked up at Shae, horrified.

She laid a hand on his shoulder. "It's okay, Mason, they're happy tears."

He glanced back at Gracie, who was still sobbing as she and hugged the dog. "Are you sure?"

"I'm sure."

Looking skeptical, Mason patted Gracie's shoulder and had just started to stand when she launched herself at him, wrapped her arms around his neck and clung tight. "Thank you, thank you, thank you. He's the best."

He hugged her back, closed his eyes and breathed in deeply the scent Shae was so familiar with.

Shae didn't bother to hold back the tears, simply let them roll down her cheeks unimpeded as father and daughter embraced each other. It might be the only chance they ever got to do so.

"I'm glad you like him, Gracie." When she stepped back, Mason took a deep breath and stood. He cleared his throat, twice. "He has a special vest to wear so he'll know when he's supposed to be working. When he's wearing the vest, you won't be able to play with him. When he's not wearing his vest, like right now, you can. You're going to have to help take really good care of him, though. He needs to be fed, and given water, and brushed."

She threw her arms around Shae. "I will. I promise."

And with that, Gracie bolted down the hallway, skidded into a U-turn and ran back toward them, all with the dog in hot pursuit.

Mason's mouth fell open as he watched them barrel through the house like it was their own personal playground. "Uh... I...uh..."

"Yup." But it didn't matter to Shae—the noise, whatever mess they might make...all that mattered to her was the pure joy radiating from her daughter. "I don't know what to say, Mason. Thank you."

"I hope it's okay. When I called Zac to try to help me put together a few things for under the tree, he said he had a K-9 dog available, newly graduated. I didn't want to wake you, but you always talked about getting a puppy, said you'd never had a pet growing up, so I just figured... Plus, I thought it might help her to have something to take care of, something that will protect her and make her feel safe... You know, with—"

"Mason." She popped up on tiptoes and kissed his cheek. "He's perfect. Thank you."

He slid an arm around her shoulders and kissed her temple. "Merry Christmas."

"Merry Christmas, Mason, and thank you for making it so special for Gracie. And for me." She leaned into his side and put her arm around his waist, enjoying the strength encircling her, then rested her head against his shoulder, letting her tension dissipate. The future might hold no hope for them, but she could at least enjoy this one moment of comfortable camaraderie.

The dog bolted full force across the living room, sprang onto the couch, hit the back cushion, twisted like an acrobat and reversed course instantly, then ran the other way, all with Gracie tagging along behind him squealing and clapping her hands. If ever there could be a perfect moment amid the recent bedlam, this was it.

Shae half wondered if he would really calm down and be a working dog when he had his vest on.

"There's something else I have to tell you," Mason said quietly.

"What's that?" Gracie and Storm were getting a little too rambunctious. She was going to have to corral them…in a minute.

"We found Lucas Gianelli—"

She stiffened. The man Mason had identified from the pageant video. That pageant seemed like a lifetime ago. "Okay."

"He's staying at a low-budget motel about twenty miles from here. I'm going to—"

"Stop." She knew exactly what was coming, and she did not want to hear it. Not now. Not today. Not ever, really, though she knew she couldn't prevent his eventual departure. "Please, Mason. Give me this one moment in time to just be happy…" *With you*, though she'd never say that part out loud. "I know it won't last, but I'm so tired, and I just need peace for a little while."

"Okay." He kissed the top of her head, then released her, the few inches now separating them seeming like a chasm the size of the Grand Canyon.

"Come on, Gracie." She forced herself to step away. He was leaving, even sooner than she'd feared. They were in danger, Gracie was in danger, and Mason was leaving. Again. The fact that he was trying to find a way to protect them, to keep Kincaid from finding them, didn't help ease the pain or the fear. Even if she didn't trust him to stay, she felt safer when he was around. "Honey, you have to stop running around now. Don't you want to open your presents?"

She skidded to a stop in front of Shae, and the dog plowed into the backs of Gracie's legs, buckled her knees and had her flopping over backward in a fit of giggles.

Shae laughed, though much of the joy that had filled her a few minutes ago had turned to dread, and helped Gracie back onto her feet. She could tell Gracie was more interested in the dog than the gifts now, so she said, "Come on, you two. Why don't we snuggle on the couch and have a story, then you can have breakfast and open the rest of your presents?"

"Okay, Mommy." She hopped onto the couch and snuggled into the corner. The dog followed, curling himself up beside her and placing his head in her lap.

Shae sat beside them as Mason lingered, arms folded, one foot crossed over the other, shoulder against the entryway wall. If possible, he seemed even more incredibly handsome than ever. She sighed and turned away. "What kind of story would you like?"

"A Christmas one."

She had to lean over the dog, who seemed very content to lie between them, to put an arm around Gracie. She began the story of baby Jesus that Gracie enjoyed so much, twisting strands of Gracie's hair between her fingers as Gracie stroked Storm's soft head. When she reached the point where Mary and Joseph arrived at the inn, Gracie interrupted.

"Mommy?"

"Yes?"

"Were there dogs at the stable when baby Jesus was born?"

She'd never thought about it before. "I think there probably were."

Her daughter looked down at Storm, wrapped her arms around him and hugged him close. "And do you think they kept baby Jesus safe so no bad people could hurt Him?"

Oh, baby. No child should have to know such fear. "I do, honey, yes."

"Will Storm keep me safe?"

Pain lanced her heart. "Yes, I think he will protect you."

She looked up at Shae, tears shimmering in her eyes, tipping over thick, dark lashes to roll down her cheeks. "And then the bad men won't be able to get us?"

"No, baby, they won't."

"Okay." Gracie crawled over Storm and lay down, lowering her head to Shae's lap. The dog rearranged himself on her other side protectively. Shae looked up to find Mason still watching them from the entryway and had no doubt he was procrastinating and should already have left to return to his undercover persona. At least this time, he'd say goodbye and take the memory of his daughter with him.

Mason pulled into the garage parking lot next to the motel where Lucas Gianelli was reportedly staying. He'd spent a tense Christmas Day with Shae, Gracie and the other agents, giving Shae the moment of rest she'd asked for, but now it was time to get back to work. He needed to resume his place in Kincaid's organization, hopefully without anyone realizing he'd disappeared for a couple of days. He usually worked dark, no contact with Zac's team for long stretches. This time, he was going in with backup. This time, he wanted to get the evidence he needed to take out the Kincaids all at once. "Testing, one, two, three."

"Gotcha, Mason," Zac responded in his earpiece. The fact that Zac had come himself meant a lot. Mason knew he was in good hands, which meant he could push Lucas harder than he might otherwise, confident Zac would know when to hang back and let things play out and when to move in if Mason got into trouble. "You're sure you're good with this, Mason?"

Was he? They'd come up with the plan in the early hours of the morning, deciding to apply pressure to Lucas in the hopes of getting enough to arrest him and then get him to flip on Sebastian. This would never work in New York, where the Kincaids had too many loyal accomplices; they could either spring Gianelli from prison or see him eliminated there. But here in Florida, there might be some small hope he'd turn against Kincaid in return for immunity or a reduced sentence. Especially if he was more loyal to Quentin than Sebastian. They could play on his fear of Sebastian, his doubt about the younger Kincaid's leadership.

So Mason had to get his head in the game. But instead of reviewing his past relationship with Lucas on the ride over, searching for weaknesses to exploit, planning ways to gain information, Mason's thoughts had been filled with Shae and Gracie, their fear like a knife in his heart as he wondered what their lives could have been like if Shae had never stumbled upon Quentin Kincaid's murder plot.

Mason shrugged off thoughts of the past. Could-haves and what-ifs would do nothing to help them now.

They said God works in mysterious ways. Mason had

fallen too far from his faith while undercover, excusing
the theft, the intimidation, the beatings, all in the name
of trying to do the right thing. He wouldn't go that route
again. If he couldn't get Kincaid without resorting to that
kind of behavior, they'd have to find another way. Seeing how Shae's faith had strengthened her, had led her
through what had to have been a difficult and frightening
six years, made him rethink the path he'd followed, the
behaviors he'd excused. It was time to return to the right
path, time to fully embrace the beliefs he'd always held.

He climbed out of the clunker he'd been driving while
undercover, which Zac had had shipped down from New
York for him. The neighborhood seemed more indus-
trial than commercial, with a row of warehouses lining
the street across from the garage. Not ideal, considering
Kincaid could have men in any of them.

Trusting Zac to take care of anything that went on
outside, he entered through the roll-up garage door.
While the Kincaids mainly ran their business out of
New York, they owned properties all over the country
to help them import and ship product as well as launder
their vast fortune.

"Hey! Anyone here?" His voice echoed through the
space, empty but for an old Cadillac on one of the lifts.
He already knew Lucas was somewhere on the premises.
Zac's agents had had him under surveillance. He strolled
through the reception area, tapped a bell sitting on the
dust-covered counter, then leaned over the counter and
yelled into the back storage room, "Hello?"

Lucas appeared from the back, amid shelving units
filled with boxes, where Mason doubted anything legal
was going on, spread his hands on the counter and rested

his considerable bulk. The rusty stains beneath his nails probably had nothing to do with fixing cars. "What's up, man?"

Only years of undercover experience allowed Mason to school his features enough to keep the absolute rage from showing. He had to stuff his hands into his pockets to stop himself from pummeling this guy at the thought of him attacking Shae and Gracie. "Hey, Luke."

Lucas narrowed his gaze. Either Mason hadn't hidden his anger as well as he'd thought or something else had raised Luke's suspicions. "Where you been, dude? Kenny's been looking for you. Said you were supposed to be down here helping with the boss's priority job."

Shae.

So much for hoping his absence hadn't been noticed. Kenny was the guy Mason usually worked with, low-level but trying hard to work his way up. If he thought for one instant Mason wasn't who he claimed to be, he'd have tripped over his own feet running to tattle to Sebastian.

He flung an arm toward the lot where he'd left the car, which was conveniently pouring smoke from its engine compartment, and let a bit of anger slip. "Car took a dump on the way down here. Been filling it with water and babying it all the way. Stupid pile of junk starts shaking every time I hit sixty and needs a break every hundred miles or so."

Lucas eyed him for a moment as if weighing the honesty in his words. He must have passed the test, because Lucas rounded the counter and led Mason through the garage and out to the lot. "Let's take a look."

"Yeah, thanks." When Lucas clapped him on the

back, Mason's skin crawled. He considered it a win when he resisted the urge to throw him to the ground and cuff him—barely. "Anything goin' on since you got down here?" At his lower level, Mason should only know there was an important job to do here, not any details.

Lucas yanked a greasy rag from the back pocket of his jeans, wiped his hands, then stuffed it back into his pocket. "Open the hood, Mace."

Mason did as instructed, loath to turn his back on Lucas but knowing Zac probably had the man in his sights. "Do I need to get up to speed on anything?"

"Are you kidding me? You think these storms have been bad…" Lucas gestured up toward the billowing, dark gray clouds stacked above them with a wary look. "That ain't nothin' compared to Kincaid's temper since last night."

Mason swallowed hard, his Adam's apple bobbing as if nervous, and added just the right combination of fear and respect to his tone. "What happened last night? He didn't notice I wasn't here yet, did he?"

"Nah. I doubt he even knows who you are, tough guy." Lucas leaned over the engine compartment, fiddled with a few things Mason didn't pay any attention to. He had no idea what Zac's guy had done to make it smoke like it was, but it didn't matter to him if the car got fixed or not. "Kincaid didn't say anything about you, but boy, was he ticked."

"About what? You guys only been down here, like, two or three days. What could have gone wrong in that short a time?" He held his breath, waited. He needed to get something. If Lucas didn't say anything to incriminate himself, they'd have to come up with another plan.

"Hey, Luke!" The front door banged shut behind a tall, rangy guy wearing a red baseball cap crammed down over a brown mop of frizz. Though Mason had never seen him before, he sort of matched the description Shae had given them of the second shooter from the pageant. The build seemed about right, and the coloring, but she'd described his hair as short. Could be it had been slicked back or tied in a tail she didn't notice. "What's going on?"

"Mace here's havin' car trouble. Just tryin' to help 'im out." Lucas pulled out the dipstick to check the oil.

"Yeah, well, Kincaid says to get back to work. He needs that stuff set up and ready to move in an hour." He gestured toward the garage, which seemed to have no actual automotive work going on but for a lone car on a lift with no tools in evidence.

"Yeah, yeah." He wiped the dipstick on the rag from his pocket, checked it and replaced it.

"Want me to help out?" Mason offered, careful not to appear too eager. "It's the least I can do, since you're fixing my car and all."

The new guy eyed Lucas as he lifted his cap, slicked his hair back, then fitted the cap back on.

"You ever worked with C-4?" Lucas asked.

Mason shrugged. "Sure."

"Whatever, then." He hooked a thumb toward the garage. "Go with Ronnie, and he'll show you what to do."

"All right." Leaving Lucas to puzzle over the car, Mason strolled into the garage with Ronnie, his mind racing. He was sure Lucas would have told him more if Ronnie hadn't shown up when he did. He paused when

Ronnie held the storage room door open. "Oh, man, hang on. I'll be right back."

"Where you going?"

He had to get back to Lucas—alone—see if he could push him into confessing to having gone after Shae. Although, if Mason wasn't successful, they might be able to get them on the C-4, if Ronnie admitted they were using it for something illegal. And since he could see no reason an automotive repair shop would need explosives, there was a good possibility they could prove that. He checked to be sure Lucas was still occupied, looked around to be sure Zac's men hadn't jumped the gun and decided to move at the mention of taking Mason into a roomful of explosives. All clear. Apparently, Zac trusted Mason to signal them if needed. "I forgot to give Lucas the key."

Ronnie shrugged and went inside, letting the door fall shut behind him.

"Did you get pictures of Ronnie?" Mason swiped a hand over his mouth to hide that he was speaking and kept his voice low as he jogged toward the car, praying Lucas wouldn't look in the ignition, where Mason had left the keys hanging, then breathed a sigh of relief when he found him still bent over beneath the hood tinkering with the engine.

"Yes. We're sending it to Angela at the safe house now to see if Shae can ID him as the second gunman," Zac said.

"All right. See if you can trace the C-4." He opened the driver's side door, palmed the keys and slid them into his pocket, then grabbed an old Coke can from the cup holder.

"Already on it."

"Thanks." Knowing who'd supplied the explosives might give them another avenue to pursue. As if in a hurry, Mason yanked the keys from his pocket. "I forgot to leave the keys."

Lucas held out his hand, and Mason tossed him the key ring, then started away. After only two steps, he turned back and snapped his fingers. "Oh, you started to say something about Kincaid being angry before, but you never finished. I wouldn't mind knowing what I'm dealing with."

"Yeah, right," he said distractedly. "He was pissed that the Bennett woman got away."

"Bennett?" Wild horses thundered in his chest.

"Avery Bennett? The chick that testified against his old man? Didn't they even tell you why they needed extra muscle down here?" He rolled his eyes, then used his coverall sleeve to wipe the sweat from his brow. "You know the old man's nearly had it, right? Well, Quentin ordered Sebastian to prove himself if he wants to take control. That's why he came down here himself. He wouldn't have bothered if we were just handling the explosives shipment."

"Oh, right. I didn't recognize the name."

"Uh-huh."

"So some chick got away all by herself?"

He stopped, then straightened and propped his hands on his hips. He aimed a hard gaze at Mason. "What's with all the questions?"

Mason shrugged. "I didn't mean nothin' by it. Just curious."

"Yeah, well, don't be." He stepped forward, pointed a

meaty finger at Mason's chest. "We've worked together before, and you're okay, so I'm gonna give you a piece of free advice. You wanna move up? There's room now, because Kincaid lost a few guys in the swamp the other night. Keep your head down, do as you're told and don't ask questions."

"Sure, man, thanks."

"Yup." He returned to work, unscrewed the radiator cap, then looked up at Mason and grinned. "And if you want to move up fast? Get the Bennett broad."

"Yeah?" His gut cramped. "Dead or alive?"

"Don't matter." He scratched his head. "Kincaid sent some of his guys after her yesterday, but it seemed she had help to escape. He went through the roof when he found out she'd slipped out of their grasp. Again. I don't think he cares so much if she's dead—that's the ultimate plan anyway—but don't kill her until you get out of her who came to her rescue last night. Otherwise, instead of moving up, you'll get buried. Kincaid thinks we got ourselves a mole." He yanked the rag out and wiped his hands. "Oh, and make sure you get her kid, too."

"There's a kid?"

"Yeah. He didn't care about her at first..." He laughed. "But I guess after he got shown up yesterday, he's gotta save face, ya know? 'Specially if he's gonna fill the old man's shoes once he croaks."

"Yeah. Got it. Thanks." Mason seethed, barely holding on to control as he nodded. "Were you in on it last night?"

He shot Mason a cocky grin. "I located her, so that saved me. Wasn't my fault those guys couldn't get hold of her when I practically ran her straight into their arms."

"Is that how it actually went down?"

"Doesn't really matter whether it did or it didn't. That's how I spun it to Kincaid, so it got me off the hook." He laughed at that. The fact that three of his comrades had ended up dead didn't seem to matter to him at all.

Mason took a swig of warm Coke as he turned away and started back toward the building, just as Ronnie stormed out of the garage. He caught sight of Mason, gritted his teeth and yanked a pistol from a holster on his hip.

"What'd you do, man? What did you do?" he screamed, spittle spraying from his mouth as he shoved the barrel of the gun hard enough against Mason's head to have him wincing and dropping the Coke as he lifted his hands in surrender. He shoved Mason backward with him as he forced him toward Lucas. "Get in the car!"

Lucas shot his hands in the air. "Whatcha doin'? What's wrong with you, Ronnie?"

"Guy's a mole, man." He tapped the barrel against Mason's head a couple of times, his face red with rage as his gaze shot from one spot to the next like a caged animal searching for escape.

Mason backed up in pace with Ronnie. He had to move, had to get that gun away from his head long enough for someone to get a shot.

Ronnie wasn't relenting. He cupped the side of Mason's head, pressed his nose practically against Mason's and jammed the weapon harder against his head. "Start talking."

EIGHT

Shae stood beside the window, off to the side so as not to make a target of herself. Not that there was much to look at, other than a patch of brittle, brownish grass surrounded by a weathered, six-foot-high stockade fence. The safe house was set against the back of the development, so beyond the fence was a sump and a brick wall. Oh, well. At least the sun had chased away enough of the clouds to uncover a patch of blue sky—for the moment.

She sighed and turned away from the window.

Gracie held a bag of training treats and commanded her new companion to sit.

He flopped down, tail wagging, and his tongue lolled out the side of his mouth.

"Good boy." Gracie popped a treat into his mouth as Mason had taught her and petted his head. When he bounced back up to lick her, she started all over again. "Good boy, Storm." She giggled. "Good boy."

Cassidy knocked on the doorjamb. "It's time for Storm's walk, Gracie."

"Can I come this time?"

Cassidy's gaze flicked to Shae, then back to Gracie. "I'm sorry, honey, but not this time."

Shae redirected her daughter's attention. "While Cassidy is walking Storm, why don't you and I go through and organize your new clothes and stuff into the bags?"

She offered a sulky shrug, head down.

Cassidy shot Shae an apologetic look as she clipped Storm's leash on and ushered him out.

"Why can't I walk him?" Gracie whined.

"We've talked about this, Gracie. It's not safe yet." Shae squatted down in front of her so they'd be eye to eye and rubbed her hands up and down Gracie's arms, which felt cold. She grabbed a sweatshirt that was hanging over the arm of a chair and held it out to her. "Here, put this on."

Gracie snatched the sweatshirt from her hand and threw it back on the chair. Then she flopped down on top of it and folded her arms across her chest in a belligerent posture Shae had no tolerance for—under normal circumstances, anyway. But these were far from normal circumstances. "I hate it here. I wanna go home."

"Gracie, please…" But what could she say to her? Shae wanted to go home, too, but Boggy Meadows was no longer home. She prayed for patience, for guidance, for some way to help her daughter cope with the reality of life on the run. But would this be her life forever? Shae had worked hard to give Gracie a happy childhood, to make her feel loved, to make her part of a community, even though the thought had frightened Shae. How long would they spend trying to outrun her past? A year? Five years? Ten?

She relaxed her shoulders, seeking to ease the tension coiled in her neck and back, concentrating on a few deep breaths so she wouldn't lose her patience and say something she'd later regret. If life on the run was the life they had, Shae would just be grateful they were alive and to-gether and make the best of a less-than-ideal situation. She picked up the new pink sequined backpack Gracie had received for Christmas. "I'm going to get us out of here as soon as I can, Gracie, but we have to be ready to go if the opportunity presents itself. So let's pack up."

She eyed Shae, seemed to be weighing her options, then finally stood, though the defiant attitude remained. "Whatever."

Figuring it was the best she was going to get, Shae held the backpack out to her. "Put this on the bed, and we'll go through your things and pack what you'd like to keep with you."

Gracie shrugged.

Ignoring the tantrum, Shae started to unpack the flight bag. While Gracie's bag would be for special things she wanted to keep with her, there was also a new duffel bag, thanks to Mason's generosity, for Shae to pack most of her own, as well as Gracie's, new clothes into. But she still needed the emergency bag, the one that had to come with them, if she was forced to leave every-thing else behind. Including Mason. Ugh…she needed to get off this emotional roller coaster.

They'd talked about a future back then, a home, a puppy. Though they hadn't yet discussed having children, in the back of Shae's mind the plan had always existed. And now here she was. Mason had popped into her life just long enough to open old wounds, bring the pain she'd managed to compartmentalize back to the forefront…and save their lives. Would she ever see him again?

She checked the time on her phone. It seemed like

he'd been gone for days, but in reality, it had only been a few hours. For all she knew, he hadn't even met up with his contacts yet. She twisted her fingers together, anxiety sending a wave of nausea crashing through her. He was fine. He'd be fine. He'd survived six years undercover. But would he disappear for another six years? Maybe show up when Gracie was going into her teens? If he ever came back.

She choked down the scream threatening to rip free. Mason might have no role in their future, but Shae still had to move forward. Mason was doing his part to protect their daughter, and she had to do her part, too. And that meant pulling herself together and getting ready to go on the run once again.

Gracie sorted through her gifts, trying to choose which things meant the most to her. She opened a small box and pulled out a charm bracelet and examined the three small charms hanging from it—a cross, a sheep that Mason had explained was to represent her part in the pageant and a heart, so she could always remember how loved she was. Most of her other gifts had been practical, like clothing and pajamas, or meant to keep her occupied, like the tablet and the coloring books and crayons. But that one had been special, meaningful, and she slid it onto her wrist before going back to her task.

Shae turned away and dumped the remainder of the flight bag onto the bed. The flash drive containing the pictures from Gracie's Christmas pageant dropped onto the top of the pile. She picked it up. "Hey, Gracie, want to see the pictures from the pageant?"

She perked up, though tears still glistened in her eyes. "Okay."

Shae opened the laptop Angela had provided, then plugged the drive in and sat down on the bed. "Come sit with me."

Gracie scrambled across the bed and snuggled into Shae's arm, a moment Shae wished could last forever. She pulled Gracie tighter against her and set the computer on her lap.

Just as pictures began to load, Cassidy returned and unleashed Storm. "Do you guys need anything else?"

"No, thank you. We're okay for now, but thank you for everything." She didn't know how they'd have made it through the past two days without the other woman's help. Not only had she been wonderful with Gracie and Storm, but she'd provided an ear in the wee hours of this morning after Mason had left, when Shae had needed someone to talk to. At least he'd stayed through Christmas day as Shae had asked.

"Of course." She smiled, emitting a warmth that soothed Shae's raw nerves. "If there's anything else you need, just let me know. Oh, and we're probably going to put together a lunch order in about an hour if you guys are hungry."

Storm launched himself onto the bed and curled against Gracie's side. Shae reached for a stuffed dog toy Gracie had left on the nightstand and handed it to him.

"Thanks." Shae waited for the door to close, then clicked on the first video. It showed Gracie dancing around the house in her pajamas two days before the pageant. She'd been so excited, her eyes filled with innocence, and love, and hope. Had some of that dimmed permanently? Shae hoped not.

The video ended, and Shae scrolled to the next picture. While Shae scrolled, Gracie narrated every step, as if Shae hadn't been present in the moment. Tension seeped from both of them, and when Gracie laughed out loud, Shae finally breathed easier. They'd be okay. Gracie would be okay. It might take some time, and the worst of it might not be over, but they'd get through it together, and they'd come out the other side stronger.

Shae swiped the tears that had tracked down her cheeks before Gracie could notice, then tapped the arrow button and brought up the next picture—Gracie at the dress rehearsal, cheek to cheek with her friend Katie, both grinning widely. The next showed an expanded view of the auditorium with Gracie and Katie striking poses on stage. Shae froze, hand hovering above the keyboard. Then she enlarged the photo.

A woman stood in the far corner of the shot, bathed in shadows but clearly watching the audience rather than the drama onstage. Even with the long, wavy locks of auburn hair partially covering her face, Shae recognized her. At least, she thought he did.

Gracie tapped her shoulder. "Mommy?"

Shae jumped out of the bed, taking the laptop with her. "Stay there with Storm, Gracie. I'll be right back. Don't move from this room."

Gracie's chin trembled as tears welled in her eyes.

"I'll be right back, baby. I promise. I just remembered I have to give Angela something really important."

Her daughter nodded and smiled a bit shakily.

Pulling the door shut behind her, Shae jogged down the hallway and found Angela and Cassidy both in the kitchen filling mugs with coffee.

Angela held up a mug. "Want some?"

"No. Thanks. Look at this." She slapped the computer down on the counter, and both women leaned over as she pointed to the image on the screen. "This was Gracie's dress rehearsal for the pageant. There were quite a few parents there, but I didn't notice this woman before. I think I recognize her. I can't be a hundred percent sure, because her face is shadowed and when I enlarge it, it gets too blurry to see clearly. Is there anything you can do to make the image clearer?"

"Give me the flash drive." Angela held out a hand. "Who do you think it is?"

Shae ejected the drive and handed it over. "I'd rather wait until I'm sure." It had been more than six years since she'd seen her, and she'd been only a teenager at that time. She'd filled out some, matured, but Shae was almost sure it was the same woman.

Angela strode in her no-nonsense way to the living room command center, sat and got to work trying to enhance the image. It didn't take long before she sat back. "That's the best I can do."

Shae studied the woman's features, now clear thanks to Angela's finessing. "That's fine."

"Who is it?"

"Regina Kincaid."

Cassidy frowned at Angela. "Regina?"

Shae was the one who answered. "Quentin's daughter. Sebastian's sister. She's quite a bit younger than he is, and while I knew Sebastian because he'd often spend time hanging around his father's office, I only met Regina once or twice."

Angela's fingers flew across the keyboard as screen after screen popped up. "We were aware he had a daughter, but she'd been dismissed long ago. She left her father's home, attended college—in California, actually—and never returned to New York. There's no record of her ever having visited him in prison, no phone calls between them that we can tell."

"So what would she be doing at Gracie's dress rehearsal?" Shae asked.

"Are you sure it couldn't have been a coincidence? Maybe she has a child in the pageant, or a relative, or a friend?" Cassidy studied the screens, speed reading through the info almost as fast as Angela could access it.

"She's not married, has no children..." Angela recited. "And she lives all the way across the country from Boggy Meadows."

"What are the chances she wasn't working for her brother?" Sweat pooled at the base of Shae's spine even as her insides went ice-cold.

Angela was already shaking her head. "Slim to none."

Cassidy paled. "So, she was already aware of your whereabouts..."

"Two days before the attack." That woman, or someone else in Kincaid's organization, had been watching Shae and Gracie, spying on them, for at least two days. The little hairs at the back of her neck stood at attention. Someone could have taken them out at any time, and Shae hadn't even been aware of the danger.

With Ronnie's weapon pressed tightly against his temple, Mason backed up. The instant his back hit the car, he slammed his head forward into Ronnie's nose. When Ronnie stumbled back, Mason shifted enough to grab hold of his wrist. He twisted, turned and snapped the bones, sent an elbow into Ronnie's throat even as he started to scream, then yanked the weapon from Ronnie's hand and tucked it into the back of his own waistband while Ronnie gasped for breath. He shoved Ronnie backward away from him, giving himself room to fight. "What is wrong with you?"

"There're cops out back," Ronnie wheezed. Blood sprayed from his nose as he spoke, giving him a nasal, whiny sound.

Mason held his breath to see if law enforcement would swarm the lot, even though he hadn't uttered the phrase that would let them know he was in trouble and summon help. Since Zac wasn't in charge of the operation, only an adviser, he didn't have the final say on when backup moved in. It could be any minute now. Mason could envision the dispute currently taking place as Zac pleaded his case, argued for them to hold off until they could ascertain the plan for the C-4. Question was, did they have all they were likely to get, or could Mason get more?

Cradling his wrist, Ronnie turned on Lucas. "This is your fault. You brought him in, and I'm going to make sure Kincaid knows it."

"What are you talking about? He's Kenny's guy. He's worked for Kincaid for years. I worked with him in New York. Whatever you think you know, you're wrong." Lucas leveled Mason with a look that said he'd better be right.

Before Mason could reply, the world exploded into chaos around them as Zac's men, along with the FBI and local law enforcement, moved in. He didn't blame them, even agreed they weren't likely to get anything

more after Ronnie had spotted the police setting up behind the garage. Sloppy work on the part of the officers
posted out back? Or had he received a warning from
someone in law enforcement who was loyal to Kincaid?
Either way, someone had apparently deemed the information he had been able to record enough to bring the
two in for questioning. Of course, Ronnie would need
a detour to the hospital for treatment first.

Zac grabbed Mason roughly by the arm and whirled
him toward the car, gun steadily aimed at his head. Even
if Lucas and Ronnie were going to jail, it was important
to maintain his cover.

"Let go of me!" Mason yelled, yanking his arm away.

"Hands on the car!" Zac shoved him face first toward
the vehicle, nudging his feet apart with his boot. "Now!"

Mason leveled a glare at Lucas. If he could cause dis-
sension among Kincaid's men, one of them might roll
more easily. "What's going on here, Luke? You some
kinda rat or something?"

"What?" His eyes went wide, mouth dropping open.
"Don't you try to pin this on me, dude."

Mason fought back a grin at the sheer terror written
on the other man's face. Zac would have a field day with
him if whoever ended up with jurisdiction allowed him
to interrogate the guy. Thankfully, the FBI and local police were cooperating, had even allowed Jameson Investigations' agents access to this scene. In the meantime,
Mason would just plant some seeds for Lucas to nurture
for a little while. He raised his voice so Ronnie, who was
being led out of the parking lot in cuffs, would be sure to
hear. "When Kincaid finds out you were working with
the feds, you're done, man."

Zac shoved Mason toward his waiting SUV, covered his head and wrestled him inside as Mason continued to resist. When the back door finally closed and Zac jumped into the front seat, they waited and watched as the two suspects were loaded into separate vehicles and the raid on the garage began.

"They know about the explosives?" He didn't want the cops to walk into a storage room full of C-4 with no prior knowledge.

"Yeah."

Mason used the key Zac had pressed into his hand while wrestling him into the car to unlock the cuffs behind his back. He rubbed his wrists and handed the cuffs and key over the seat to Zac. "Did Shae ID the second suspect?"

"No. Angela said she wasn't sure. She thought it might be Ronnie but couldn't be sure from the picture. We're going to pick her up and bring her in with us, see if she can ID him in a lineup." Zac turned to face him. "They did find something else, though."

"What's that?"

"Regina Kincaid. You know her?"

"The sister? No. I've never met her." If he recalled correctly, she was much younger than Sebastian, probably only in her early to mid-twenties now, and not in the picture. He tried to think back, remember what he'd heard about her, couldn't come up with anything more. "As far as I know, she wasn't involved with the business."

"Hmm..." Zac quirked a brow at him. "So what reason would she have had to be at Gracie's dress rehearsal on Wednesday night?"

None. Mason hadn't even known about the danger

then. She shouldn't have been there. The fact that she was, and hadn't managed to ding anyone's radar, disturbed him. "Where is she now?"

Zac lifted his hands, let them drop, then turned back around and started the SUV. He shifted into Reverse, then hooked his arm over the passenger seat and looked over his shoulder. "Right now, finding her is a priority."

"Hang on, Zac." Mason needed to be at the police station to at least witness Lucas's interrogation, but he didn't trust anyone else to take Shae to the hospital to see if she could ID Ronnie. "Do me a favor?"

He stepped on the brake, hesitated before shifting into Drive. "What's that?"

"You have security at the hospital?"

"Of course."

"Your own?" Mason wished he could trust the FBI and the local police, but an FBI agent had given them up six years ago and had cost Marty his life. He wasn't taking any chances with Shae. Quentin Kincaid had his hands in too many high-ranking pockets. And those who weren't on the take could be threatened, coerced or even disappeared.

Zac nodded. "In addition to other agencies, yes."

"All right. I'll go pick Shae up and bring her to the hospital. I understand we'll have to do an official lineup afterward, but it would be helpful if we knew if he was the second gunman as soon as possible. In the meantime, can you go ahead to the station? I'd like you to be there in case Lucas starts talking."

"All right. Sure." Zac double-checked that the cars carrying both suspects had left the parking lot and disappeared from sight, then shifted into Park and climbed out. "You take the SUV. I'll get a ride with one of the others."

Mason hopped out and slid into the driver's seat. "Thanks, Zac."

"You bet. And Mason? Be careful. When Sebastian finds out two more of his men have been picked up, he's going to lose his mind. And if he gets an attorney in to talk to them and finds out we raided the garage right after you showed up…"

"Yeah. I get it. It won't take him long to put two and two together. As soon as they determine I'm no longer in custody, he'll figure I'm the mole, even if he doesn't know I was in Florida when Shae went on the run. I'll be careful." As careful as he could be, anyway. But what did that mean for his undercover work? Unless he could come up with a valid excuse to explain how he'd escaped custody, his time in the Kincaid organization was over. So where did that leave him? With no future? Back at the FBI? Continuing to work with Jameson Investigations? He had no idea, and the tension was turning into a dull throb in his head. Better to think about this some other time.

While he drove, he called ahead to let Shae know he was on his way to pick her up. Angela answered and went to retrieve her. Even with guards posted at the hospital, being there would still be the most dangerous part of the excursion.

She answered breathlessly. "Mason?"

"Shae, listen, I'm almost there to pick you up. I need you to come ID someone at the hospital."

"The hospital? Are you—"

"I'm fine. The guy I put in there might be less fine.

And…there's something I need to discuss with you."

Something she wasn't going to like.

"Okay."

"First off, the weather is brutal. Storms are picking up again, and they've already spawned two tornadoes that I know of."

"Yeah. It was sunny here for a few minutes, but it's raining buckets again now."

"Shae, you know I'll do everything I can to keep you safe. Plus, you already proved in the swamp that you know how to handle yourself, and still…"

"If Kincaid's men show up at the hospital, there could be another shootout," she finished for him.

"Yes." And since the younger Kincaid seemed even less concerned about collateral damage than his father, he'd think nothing of sending men to kill Ronnie to keep him quiet. And if they stumbled across Shae at the hospital… But how could he suggest what he knew needed to be said? He ran it through a million ways in his head.

"You want me to leave Gracie here."

He blew out a pent-up breath. Shae didn't miss a beat. "It's your decision, but I think it would be safer for her to remain at the safe house with Angela and the FBI agents on duty."

Silence hummed over the line.

He listened to the rain pound against the SUV's steel roof.

"Angela has to go out for something," she finally said.

"When?"

"I'm not sure. Now, I think."

"I'm almost there, Shae. What do you want to do?"

She groaned, clearly warring over the decision. "All right. I'll leave Gracie here."

"Meet me at the front door in two minutes. Don't come out until I get to the door." He'd pull the SUV onto the lawn if he had to, just to get as close as possible to the front door. "Put Angela on."

"All right. I'll be ready."

"Yeah, Mason," Angela answered a moment later.

"Shae said you're leaving?"

"Just for about an hour. I have to follow up on something."

"Who's there?"

"Ronaldo, Monroe, Jenkins, and Leroy."

"You trust them?"

"Zac's worked with Jenkins and Leroy. Jimmy Ronaldo and Cassidy Monroe are new to us, but they've been vetted."

Not ideal, but at least Gracie and Cassidy had bonded over taking care of Storm. He might as well accept the fact that he wasn't going to be comfortable leaving Gracie no matter what. But it wasn't safe to take her, and they needed that ID. They had to know if one of the gunmen was still on the loose. "All right. I'm pulling in now."

He disconnected and pulled onto the lawn with the passenger-side door lined up with the front porch. The fewer people who saw Shae, the better, plus this would protect her from the weather.

Unease sat in his gut like a lead weight as he ran to the door, then guided Shae back to the SUV, shut the door behind her and pulled out. "You doing okay?"

She hesitated. "Yes."

"Shae…"

"I'm okay. I'll just feel better once we're back here, especially if I know you have both shooters in custody." She turned to face him. Dark circles sat under her eyes. Stress lines bracketed her mouth. "I'm sure Kincaid has more gunmen. They won't take away Gracie's protection just because these two were apprehended, right?"

"You and Gracie will have protection until there's no longer a threat, and we can set you up with a new identity, somewhere far from both New York and Florida."

She turned her gaze away and nodded, but not before he noted the flash of pain in her eyes.

"I'm sorry, Shae, but it won't be safe for you to return to Boggy Meadows." And it was a shame, because it seemed Shae and Gracie had both thrived there. "You know that."

"I do." She nodded. "Yes."

"But I promise you, when it's safe to do so, I'll find a way to get anything of importance from your old life to you."

"I already have the most important things with me." Her gaze turned to him, then her eyes widened and color flared in her cheeks. "I…um… I wouldn't mind having Gracie's baby things and a box of her artwork."

"Okay. I'll take care of it." Ignoring whatever that slip might have meant, he kept his eyes on the road ahead of him as the intensity of the storm increased. Hail began to pelt them. The windshield wipers couldn't keep up, reducing visibility to almost nothing. He lifted his foot off the gas some, slowing them to a fast roll. When his phone rang, he hit the button to answer it on the car speaker. "Yeah?"

"Where are you?" Zac asked.

He sensed the anger emitting from him in waves. "On my way to the hospital. Why?"

"Lucas Gianelli escaped."

"What! How could that happen, Zac? Who was transporting him?" Because if it was the FBI agents, he was turning around and going back for Gracie. He eased off the gas even more, searched for somewhere to pull over, squinting to see through the storm. He could barely tell where the road was.

"Two officers from the local police, followed by two FBI agents. All four are dead."

"Ah, man." Though losing four officers brought a wave of grief, as least none of them had been involved with Kincaid. If they had, they would still be alive. "You have enough guards on Ronnie?"

"Yeah. They won't get to him."

A bolt of lightning hit so close he could almost feel the sizzle.

Shae squealed, startled.

"What's happening, Mason?"

"Just some really intense lightning and an almost constant rumble of thunder." The roar increased until it was nearly deafening. He pulled back out onto the narrow two-lane road.

"Where are you?"

"I'm about to pull into the hospital parking lot, but visibility is awful. I'm navigating by GPS at this point."

"All right, I'm right behind you. I'll meet you there in about five minutes."

"Sounds good." He disconnected the call. The lot had already begun to flood as he searched for a spot near the hospital entrance. Nothing, and he didn't want to block the ambulance bay or the drop-off and pickup lanes. Resigned to dashing through the storm, he grabbed a spot in the middle of the parking lot as someone else backed out. "You ready?"

She looked up at the sky, then at him, and lifted a brow. "As I'll ever be, I guess."

"Sit right there until I come around." He inhaled deeply, shook off the desire to remain right where he was in the SUV with her and listen to the storm rage, and shoved open the door. "Let's do this."

He hopped out, automatically scanning for trouble as he rounded the front of the vehicle and opened the door for Shae. After waiting for her to emerge, he slammed the door shut and took her hand. "Come on."

The windshield of the Volkswagen beside him exploded beneath a barrage of automatic weapon fire.

NINE

"Get down!" Mason shoved Shae to the ground, whipped his pistol from its holster and pressed his back against the SUV. He had to realize they couldn't stay there. They had to move. "Go around the back of the Volkswagen."

Keeping in a crouch, she did as he said, sensing him following right on her heels. Where had the shots come from? She hadn't been able to tell.

"Shae? You okay?" Mason's voice called from her left.

She took stock for a moment. Other than some nausea and a pounding headache, she seemed to be in one piece. "I think so. Are you hurt?"

"No. I'm fine."

She turned her head to face him.

Blood streamed from his temple as he tapped his earpiece, the wound he'd sustained in the swamp having reopened. "We're taking fire."

"Two minutes out."

"Got it." Mason stood, still stooped over, and glanced through the Volkswagen's back window toward the hospital. He rested a hand on her shoulder. "Stay down. Everything will be fine. We'll have help in a minute."

So why did his tone hold such urgency? What wasn't he telling her? "Is something else wrong?"

"Nothing specific. I just feel like a sitting duck here. We need to get away from the vehicle."

"Okay." He was right, especially since they couldn't see much of anything surrounding the vehicle, the position they'd taken cover in allowing no view. "Make sure you're not hurt. I don't want to start running and find out you're injured."

She did as instructed, taking inventory from head to toe. A few aches and pains, but nothing serious. She could run if they got a chance. She turned her attention to the cut on his temple. "You're bleeding a lot."

"It's fine. Nothing serious. It just grazed me." He swiped at the blood with the back of his hand as if it were a simple annoyance.

"Grazed? You mean you were shot?" Shae's voice rose to near hysterical, but she couldn't control it. Nor could she control the tremors coursing through her. Mason had been shot. In the head. A fraction of an inch over and he'd be dead. She started to hyperventilate.

"Hey. Look at me." Mason squatted in front of her, cupped her face. "Listen to me. I'm fine. It probably just reopened the stitches Doc Rogers put in." He grinned. "I'm gonna have to listen to a lecture about that later when he restitches me."

She shoved his hand away. "How can you joke about that?"

"I'm sorry, Shae. And trust me, I already said a prayer of thanks, but I'm okay." He shifted his gaze from their surroundings to stare into her eyes. "And we have to move. We can't stay here."

"Okay." She nodded, willing her heart back down from her throat, then swiped away tears and rain. "Okay. I'm sorry. I'm okay."

"You have nothing to be sorry for."

She had to get a grip. "C-c-could you tell where they were shooting from?"

His gaze lingered on her for another moment, then he returned to scrutinizing the lot. "The direction of the hospital, but I'm not sure where."

"How are we going to get out of here?"

He gripped her hand, lending her strength she was sorely lacking at the moment. "When I say go, I want you to stay low and head to the right. Stay behind the cars as much as possible, and when you come to that van at the end, crouch low and stay behind the back tire. Okay?"

"Yeah. Okay. Got it."

"Ready?"

She shifted, getting into a better position to push off. "Yeah."

Mason grabbed a half-full soda bottle someone had dropped in the parking lot, stood higher and tossed it in the opposite direction. "Go!"

Shots took out another windshield in the direction he'd thrown the bottle.

Shae held her breath, kept her head low and ran without looking back. When she reached the black van, she ducked behind the back bumper, careful to keep the tire directly in front of her.

Mason held his weapon in a two-handed grip, firing as he ran behind her. He reached her just as an SUV fishtailed into the lot and sped in the direction of the hospital. "I got one of them, but there's still at least one more. Zac and his guys are going after him now. Are you hurt?"

"No, I'm good. Just shaken up."

"Okay. We're going to sit tight until Zac gives the all clear."

She nodded, sucked in a deep breath and crouched to sit on the rain-slicked ground, then leaned her back against the van's bumper. Her legs were shaking too badly to hold her.

"It'll be okay, Shae. Zac had men already in the hospital to help comb the area."

"This is so ridiculous." She wrapped her arms around her legs and lowered her head to her knees, then started to laugh.

He frowned at her as if she'd finally crumbled beneath the pressure.

And she sighed. "Did you ever get the feeling you weren't meant to do something? It's like every step of the way, hurdles are thrown into our paths."

"When that happens, I usually sit back and reassess what I'm doing. I used to pray for guidance and direction, but I'm ashamed to admit it's been a long time since I've done so."

She turned her head so she could see him but kept her cheek resting on her knees. "Why?"

"I don't know. I guess I just kind of gave up after Marty was killed, after I had to leave you to go undercover…" He looked away, probably somewhere in the past. "It was the most difficult decision I've ever made, Shae. But it was something I had to do. I was a coward to leave without saying goodbye to you, without letting you know what was going on, without at least offering some explanation after everything that happened. I think I was afraid to see you, afraid you'd ask me to stay."

"And you couldn't." She understood now why he'd had to leave, just not why he'd done so without an explanation.

"No. That's just it." He paused midsearch. "I would have. *And* I couldn't."

"It's okay, Mason. It's in the past now, and when Gracie and I needed you most, you came back." She gripped his hand, willed him to believe what she was saying. "And that's all that matters."

"Thank you," he said softly.

"Now." She smiled. "If you can find any room in your heart for faith, a prayer right now probably wouldn't hurt."

He grinned back at her. "I'll see what I can do." Then he paused and raised a hand to his earpiece, listening. "Ten-four."

She shot him a questioning look.

"We're all clear. They've got two shooters in custody." He stood, stretched his back and held out a hand to Shae.

Grateful, Shae took his hand and let him help her up, then looked around the lot and moved closer to him.

He lay an arm across her shoulders, tilting his head so it leaned against hers, but she could sense his tension. "You okay?"

"Yes." And it was time to move. She didn't need Mason to tell her standing out there in the open was akin to painting a target on their backs. "Let's go. But, Mason?"

"Yeah." He gripped her hand.

"I'll take a look at the guy you want me to ID, and

then we need to reassess our course of action." She gestured toward the shattered windshields. "Clearly this is
not working. They keep finding us. I think maybe we're
missing something, and we need to slow down for a minute and figure out what."

He nodded and kept her beneath his arm as they
walked toward the hospital, but he didn't holster his
weapon.

As she surveyed the damage to the vehicles, more
than she'd realized from her crouched position, she offered a silent prayer of thanks that they'd survived and
that she hadn't left Gracie alone in the world.

"Mason?"

"Yeah."

"I need you to promise me something." Because there
was no one she'd trust with this more.

"What's that?"

She hesitated, waited until he stopped walking and
turned to her, then squeezed his hand. "I want you to
promise if anything happens to me, you'll take care of
Gracie."

His breath whooshed out in one long rush. "Shae,
I—"

"Please. We've been in witness protection her whole
life. I left everyone who was once a part of my life behind and never trusted anyone to forge a relationship
close enough that I'd trust them with my daughter's life."
She squeezed his hand tighter, willed him to understand
the importance of her request, the amount of trust she
was placing in him. Did she hope for something more
with him when all this was said and done? She had no
idea, couldn't think past the here and now, but she did

trust him with Gracie. Of that, she was certain. "Please, Mason. I need to know she'll be taken care of by someone who will love her and would risk his life to protect her, just like I would."

He closed his eyes, lowered his head and pressed their joined hands against his forehead, then rocked his head back and forth in a gesture she feared was refusal.

The sound of a vehicle approaching interrupted, and she figured he'd use the excuse for a reprieve. Maybe she'd overestimated his feelings for Gracie. She slid her hand out of his. "It's okay, Mason. I'm sorry. I shouldn't have asked. I didn't mean to put you on the spot."

He looked up at her then, and tears mixed with the rain dripping down his face. "Shae. I will take care of Gracie. You have my word that if anything…happens to you, I will take care of her. I will raise her to be a good, loving, faithful person, just like her mother. But nothing will happen to you, Shae, because I won't allow it. I can't."

When he cupped her cheek, she leaned into the warmth of his hand. "Thank you."

"Mason!" Zac called as he swung the door of the SUV open. "Get in."

Mason squeezed his eyes closed for a moment, then pressed his lips against Shae's forehead, held her that way for a moment, then released her.

Zac and Angela were in the front seats, so Shae and Mason climbed into the back.

"You two okay?" Zac asked.

"Yeah."

"Angela was just heading back to the safe house, but I told her to ride with me. This weather is brutal." He eyed Shae in the rearview mirror. "Did you really have to pick an El Niño winter to get found during?"

A smile tugged at her. "Sorry. I'll try to do better next time."

"See that you do." He winked at her in the mirror, then pulled up to the ambulance entrance. "Do you still want to go into the hospital?"

Mason glanced at Shae, and she nodded once. "Let's just get this done. I wasn't able to ID him from the pictures, but he looks familiar. There's something about him that I can't place, but I know I've seen him before. I'm pretty sure if I see him in person I'll recognize him."

"You don't think he's the second gunman?"

Did she? She'd recognized the picture they'd sent of Lucas Gianelli instantly. He was one of the two who had found her at the pageant. But the other guy? She knew him. She was sure of that. But from where? Granted, she'd been under a tremendous amount of pressure and stress, but then why had she recognized the first shooter so easily? At Mason's suggestion, she'd tried to envision Ronnie with his mass of frizzy hair tied or slicked back, without the baseball cap, wearing a suit. He'd advised her to close her eyes and envision him, to let her thoughts wander and see what came to her. But so far, nothing had worked.

It wasn't until they were outside the private hospital room and she peeked through the small window that recognition slammed through her. She gasped and stumbled back from the door.

"What?" Mason frowned. "You recognize him?"

"Y-yes." Bile surged up her throat, and her knees buckled.

Mason caught her before she could hit the floor. "Get a chair."

Angela dragged a chair from across the hall to them, and Mason lowered Shae into it and guided her head between her knees. Angela held a hand up to still the two confused agents standing guard on either side of the door.

Mason kept his hand on her head. "Who is he, Shae?"

"His name isn't Ronnie. At least, that's not how I knew him."

"Who is he?" Zac stood over her, phone held ready to move as soon as she made the ID.

She had to pull herself together. Slowly, she lifted her head, controlled her breathing and forced the nausea down. There was no time to fall apart. She had to get back to Gracie. "His name is Mathew Harris, and he was an assistant coach on Gracie's soccer team last year. She didn't have much interaction with him, and I didn't have reason to pay much attention to him, but I recognize him now."

Mason's eyes went ice-cold.

"Do you think Kincaid knew where Shae was even then, or do you think it was a coincidence?" Angela asked.

"No, it's no coincidence." Zac dialed and pressed the phone against his ear. "I think Sebastian Kincaid found them a long time ago, and he was just waiting for his old man to give the order before he made his move."

"But why?" Angela glanced toward the window as if the answers might be written there.

"Who knows?" Mason lay a hand on Shae's shoulder. "Maybe Quentin wouldn't sanction the hit for some reason. Or maybe Sebastian was waiting to use the hit as a power play, even before his father asked him to prove he's a strong enough leader."

Shae started for the door. "I need to get to my daughter. Now."

Mason fishtailed around the corner and sped toward the safe house with Zac and Angela right behind them. After Shae had ID'd Mathew Harris, aka Ronnie, they'd tried to contact the agents at the safe house. None of them had answered.

Shae's hands shook wildly as she tried Cassidy Monroe's number again. "Please, answer. Please, answer."

Mason didn't tell her not to bother. It was obvious something had gone wrong and no one was going to answer their calls, but having something to concentrate on beside her daughter's fate would help keep her grounded.

She dropped the phone onto her lap and scrubbed her hands over her face. "Still no answer. How could this have happened?"

Mason didn't know what to say. His only thoughts were on Gracie—his daughter—a fact that had punched through him the instant he'd realized something had gone wrong at the safe house. She was his child, his responsibility, and he had failed her repeatedly. He'd abandoned her mother, no matter the circumstances, when she'd needed him most. He'd let Sebastian's men get close days—no, at least a year—before anyone even realized they'd located Shae. He hadn't been fast enough, had left them to be terrorized for the past few days instead of getting away cleanly. He would not fail this child, *his* child, again.

He took the next turn way too fast for the slick conditions, skidding as he struggled to regain control.

Shae braced her hands against the dashboard, clenched her teeth together and said nothing.

As the safe house came into sight, he prayed fervently, begged for Gracie's well-being. Maybe the problem was with the phone service. The storms could have caused some kind of interference. Or maybe Cassidy or one of Zac's agents had managed to get Gracie to safety but didn't have their phones with them. Or maybe Gracie had managed to run or hide. They'd alerted local law enforcement, but no one had gotten back to them yet.

He surged between two patrol cars parked at awkward angles in the street, over the curb and onto the lawn.

Shae had the door open before he fully stopped.

"Shae, wait!" He shoved the car into Park, then jumped out and ran, easily overtaking her before they reached the porch. He grabbed her arm and shoved her against the wall to the side of the front door, then pressed his own back against the wall. "Stay there."

Zac leaned against the wall on the other side, Angela next to him, all of them with weapons drawn.

The sound of Storm barking frantically, scratching against something, reached them through the open front door. The dog was still alive, that was something. But one of Zac's agents lay across the entryway. A police officer lay a few feet beyond him in the foyer. "You stay right there, Shae. You'll only be in the way and could get caught in the cross fire and get Gracie hurt. You hear me?"

She nodded, lower lip trembling. She vibrated with adrenaline, but she stayed put.

Mason crouched low. With Zac covering him from behind and Angela standing guard at the door and protecting Shae, he checked both downed officers for any sign of life, then shook his head and moved forward. Jimmy Ronaldo lay half in the kitchen, half in the hallway, no weapon in sight. Knowing it was too late to help him, Mason turned into the living room where the command center had been set up and found Zac's remaining two agents. Both dead, one in the chair in front of his computer with his weapon still holstered at his side, the other lying on the floor beside the printer with papers scattered around him. Clearly, neither had seen the attack coming. Which meant they'd known their attacker. They had to have. No way could a stranger have gotten in without the guard noticing, sneaked up on two agents and killed them before they could even draw their weapons. No, this had happened quickly, *tap-tap, tap-tap* and done. A growing feeling of dread settled in his stomach.

The dog barked and howled, trying to claw and bite his way out of the bathroom where he'd been sequestered. "Gracie?" Mason called, in case she was in there, too. No answer.

Storm never would have allowed a stranger to lock him in a room. Again, he must have known the attacker. Trust them enough to let them lock him in a room without Gracie. A suspicion was growing inside him.

Mason tuned out the dog's cries. They had to clear the house before they could do anything for him, even if he knew they wouldn't find Gracie—or Agent Cassidy Monroe.

He eased around the corner into the kitchen and found another police officer down. He felt for a pulse. Nothing. He tamped down every last emotion as he and Zac moved through the house together.

"Here…"

Mason almost missed the barely audible croak. He stopped, listened, then moved into the bedroom.

A police officer lay on the floor by the bed, bleeding profusely from a gunshot wound in his gut.

Zac whipped out his radio and called for backup as Mason grabbed a stack of towels and washcloths from the bathroom and began to administer first aid. "Can you tell me what happened, Officer…?"

"Gibbons…sir," he wheezed.

"Okay, you just hold on, Gibbons. Help's coming. You hear me?"

He nodded, sucked in a deep breath and coughed. "Girl. Didn't see her."

"When you got here?" Mason folded a towel into a compress and pressed it hard against the officer's wound. "Gracie was already gone?"

He nodded, struggled for air. "Outside, guard down in back. We came in, knew it was a child in danger, didn't wait for backup…"

"There was a female FBI agent present. Cassidy Monroe. Did you find her here?"

He shook his head and wheezed deeply. His eyes fluttered closed. "Woman shooter."

"You hold on, Gibbons. You hear me?"

And then Angela was beside him. She dropped to her knees and started chest compressions. "Ambulance is only a few minutes out. The house is clear."

"Monroe?" Rage boiled. She'd befriended Shae. And Gracie. They'd trusted her.

Angela shook her head. "I'm sorry."

He swiped a hand over his mouth, had to get to Shae. Leaving Angela to care for Officer Gibbons, he walked into the living room to find Shae sitting on the floor in the corner beside Storm, hugging the dog against her chest as she worked to soothe him.

She looked up when Mason walked in. "Gracie's not here."

"No, Shae. I'm sorry." He crouched in front of her. "We're going to find her. Do you hear me?"

Deep, racking sobs shook her as she rocked back and forth, clutching the dog. "You have to find her, Mason. You have to find my baby. Please. Oh, God, please."

He reached for her, but she yanked her arm away from him and stood.

"How could this happen?" she screamed. "How could you let this happen? I trusted you. You promised you'd keep my baby safe."

Storm stood protectively between them, eyeing Mason like he might be the villain.

"I know, Shae. I'm so sorry." No one was more furious than he was. How had he missed it? Cassidy had been so convincing, so enamored with Gracie and Storm. Of course she was. It let her lock the dog away so he didn't make a fuss while she quietly escorted the trusting child out the front door. But someone must have noticed something wrong, because she'd had to shoot her way out.

"Is she even still alive?" Shae wrapped her arms around herself and bent over. "Do you think that woman k-k—"

"No. Shae, you can't think like that." He gripped both

her arms and forced her upright. "Listen to me. Gracie is alive. Do you hear me? If they were going to kill her, they'd have had no reason to remove her from the premises. She'd be here, Shae. She's alive. Okay? And we are going to do everything in our power to figure out where she is and bring her home safe."

"You find her. You find my child right now." She turned away from him then, tremors coursing through her body as she walked to the window and looked out.

Mason lowered his head to his hand, allowing the grief to flow through him for one long moment. And then he shut everything down. Just like he'd learned to do six years ago when he'd had to walk away from Shae. He shut off everything inside him, all the pain, all the anger, all the fear, even all the love, and he turned and walked out.

He found Zac standing on the front lawn watching paramedics load Gibbons into an ambulance, one phone pressed against his ear as he tapped and scrolled on another.

"Gibbons?" Mason asked.

"They said he should make it, but we won't know for sure until they get him into surgery."

Mason nodded. One more thing he couldn't do anything about right now except to pray he'd recover. "Monroe?"

"We have an APB out. Angela's inside now trying to find out more."

He left Zac to coordinate the search effort and stalked through the house to the bedroom, where he found Angela at a desk with a laptop in front of her, eyes red and puffy as she sniffled and fought for control.

"Anything?" he asked.

"You're not going to like it."

"I don't like any of this. Tell me." Fear tried to breach his barriers, but he ignored it. It would do him no good. The anger was tougher to rein in.

"Cassidy Monroe was handpicked for this assignment by a supervisor who called out sick right after assigning her." She looked up at him, sniffed. "Local police just found his body."

Mason exploded, swung and knocked a box of tissues off the desk and across the room. "How could that have happened? Didn't anyone notice he was missing?"

Angela shook her head, unfazed by the outburst. "He called out sick, Mason. And no one had any reason to suspect Monroe. She's never been convicted of a crime, had no involvement in the Kincaid organization that I can even find after the fact. No one had any reason to look at her. She passed the background check with flying colors."

"All right. So, she's either in collusion with the Kincaids or they coerced her in some way." He huffed out a breath, raked a hand through his hair. Raging about past mistakes would do nothing to help find Gracie. "Do you have any leads?"

"Maybe." She hit a few keys, then got up and hurried to the printer. She turned and held out a page. "Her vehicle. We have it on a traffic camera getting on the turnpike heading south about fifteen minutes ago. Zac's coordinating a team."

"Thanks." Mason grabbed the page from her and took off. He'd let Shae know they had a lead, and then he'd go after Gracie himself. He strode into the living room and stopped short. She wasn't there, and a visibly agitated Storm was being leashed by a nervous agent. "Shae?"

Zac rounded the corner at a full run. "The SUV you were driving is gone."

"What?"

"One of the local officers said he saw a woman matching Shae's description take off in it about three minutes ago. He didn't know who she was, but she came from inside the house, so he had no reason to try to stop her."

"Where would she have gone?" It didn't make sense. The command center in the safe house was the first place information about Gracie would come in. It was her best chance at knowing right away if her daughter was found. "Why would she leave?"

"Unless…" Zac whirled and started for the door with Mason on his heels.

"Someone contacted her."

"Angela," Zac yelled. "Can you track Shae's cell phone?"

Mason held his breath as she accessed the information on one of the living room computers.

"It's…" She frowned and looked around the room. "It should be in here."

Mason searched in the direction she'd indicated. He found the phone stuffed beneath a chair cushion. He swiped the screen and read the text sent from Cassidy's cell phone out loud. "'We'll trade. You for Gracie. Say nothing. Leave your phone behind. Drive south on the turnpike until we intercept you.'"

Zac took the phone from him before he could throw it across the room and handed it to Angela. "Use satellites or traffic cameras, whatever you have to do, but find the vehicle Mason was driving. It left here about four minutes ago."

"Got it."

Mason had never felt so helpless as he strode toward Zac's Jeep, praying he'd find Shae and Gracie in time. His heart stopped when he found Mr. Cuddles lying beside the driveway. He bent and picked him up, pressed his face into the stuffed bunny. The tidal wave of emotions he'd so carefully suppressed broke free and inundated him.

TEN

Shae drove a steady sixty miles an hour in the right lane of the turnpike. She had no idea how Cassidy planned to intercept her, but she would make it as easy as she could. She didn't regret leaving the safe house. She had to save Gracie, and there were so few people she could trust. She did wish she'd been able to say goodbye to Mason, but he would have tried to stop her. She rubbed her chest to ease the ache there, swallowed hard to clear the lump from her throat. Was this how he'd felt when he'd left her six years ago?

It didn't matter now. Even if she wasn't about to die, there was no future for her, Gracie and Mason as a family. While she couldn't deny that she loved him with all her heart, it would never work between them. Mason was a field agent, whether he returned to the FBI or stayed with Jameson Investigations. There would always be the possibility he'd walk out again, go undercover for extended periods of time, be in danger like this on a regular basis.

So who would take care of Gracie once Shae traded herself for her daughter? She dismissed the thought—had to if she was going to make it through this. Mason might not be able to take care of Gracie himself, but Shae had no doubt he'd see to it she was cared for and loved. Zac Jameson certainly had the resources to make that happen. She shoved the thought of Gracie being raised by strangers into some deep compartment in her heart. At least her daughter would live.

An SUV pulled along Shae in the middle lane. The passenger, a guy she immediately recognized as the second gunman, gestured for her to follow.

She nodded, allowing the driver room to pull in front of her. "Mommy's coming, Gracie. This will all be over soon, and you'll be safe. I promise."

She exited the turnpike and followed the other SUV down a narrow dirt road. Trees that looked like they'd stood undisturbed for hundreds of years packed together in a thick, never-ending expanse of forest. Miles passed as her heart rate slowed. Cassidy would let Gracie go once Shae turned herself over. The woman knew Gracie, had taken care of her. She wouldn't let her die. What kind of monster would do that? Shae would convince her to drop Gracie off at a police station or a hospital or a church, somewhere she'd be safe and get help.

She prayed Gracie wasn't hurt, prayed she'd understand Shae would never leave her if there was any other choice. Surely Mason would make sure Gracie knew how much her mother had loved her. She tilted her head back and forth, easing the tension coiled in her neck. It was almost over. Once they had Shae, Gracie would no longer be in danger.

Ten miles into the woods, she entered a clearing. The lead SUV parked in front of a large cabin, probably used for hunting—or other, less legal, activities. As she looked around, she wondered how many bodies were buried in these woods and knew she'd soon join them. "God, please give me the strength to do what I need to do here. Don't let me falter."

Leaving the keys in the ignition, she got out of the SUV.

The second gunman from the pageant approached. "Face the car, hands on the roof."

She complied, let him frisk her in search of weapons or a wire, neither of which she had.

He stepped back and loosely aimed his weapon in her direction, used it to gesture toward the cabin. "Inside."

She hurried up the three steps to the front porch, registering several shadowy men there. Before she could pause, the door swung open. Cassidy Monroe ushered her inside and slammed the door behind the man who'd led her in. "Anyone follow her?"

"No. She did as you said, just ran out and drove away. No one followed."

"Good. Wait outside. Let me know immediately if anyone shows up."

He left without a word.

"How could you do this?" Shae struggled to control the anger. This woman knew her, knew Gracie, and she'd betrayed them. Confronting her would do nothing, though. She needed to get Gracie to safety first. Maybe there would be time after to say her piece. "Where's my daughter?"

Cassidy gestured toward a closed door across the large, open main room.

Ignoring her, Shae crossed the floor, then had to wait for Cassidy to unlock the door.

The instant it swung open, Shae burst through.

Her daughter lay on a cot, curled in a tight ball, shaking wildly.

"Gracie." She ran to her, scooped her into her arms and sat down on the bed when her legs gave out.

"Mommy?" She sobbed. "I knew you would come get me."

"Of course I did, baby. I'd never let anything happen to you." She only wished she could promise to stay with her always. "I love you so much, baby, more than anything in this world."

"I love you, Mommy." Gracie clung so tight Shae could barely gasp in a breath, but she just embraced her daughter, hugged her with all her might, hoping Gracie would remember this moment once Shae was gone.

"All right. Touching." Cassidy smirked. "Now, let's move."

Shae whirled on her. "You promised you'd let Gracie go if I did what you said."

"You're right." She walked across the cabin and flung the front door open, then gestured outside with the automatic weapon she held in her hand. "Get out, Gracie."

"What?" Shae lurched to her feet, Gracie clinging tightly, arms and legs wrapped around her. "You can't just throw her out in the woods."

"You want her to live?"

"Listen." Shae struggled for calm. Surely this woman could see reason. "I'll go with you without a fuss. We can drop Gracie off somewhere safe first, then I'll do whatever you want."

"Sorry, Shae, but you're not calling the shots here. And trust me…" She grinned. "You're going to do whatever I want anyway."

"She's a baby, Cassidy." They couldn't throw her out in the woods. It would be getting dark soon, and there were bears, wild boars, alligators, armed gunmen and who knew what else out there. And what if more tornadoes moved through? No way could even the most vicious woman toss a child out into the forest to survive on her own. "You can't do this. Please."

"Gracie can either walk out that front door in the next sixty seconds, or she can die here with you."

Gracie whimpered.

"I don't particularly care either way." Her grin turned feral. "Tick tock."

"You coldhearted—"

"Time's a-wasting." She glanced at her watch.

Shae lowered Gracie to the floor, crouched so she would be face-to-face with her. "Gracie, listen to me. There's a dirt road right across the clearing. I want you to follow it until you come to a paved road, then stand there and wait for a car to come by and help you. Okay?"

"No, Mommy. I can't. I'm scared. And I'm not supposed to walk on the road."

"Thirty seconds." Cassidy wagged a finger Shae was going to snap in half once her daughter was safe, even if it was the last thing she did.

"Gracie, do what I'm telling you. Right now." Shae stood and started ushering Gracie toward the door. "Cheesemonkey, okay?"

"But what about you?"

"Don't worry about me, honey. I'll be fine. I'll catch up to you as soon as I can. But you have to go now."

Gracie threw her arms around Shae's legs and sobbed.

"No, Mommy. Please don't make me. I don't wanna do cheesemonkey anymore."

"Gracie." Shae held her arms. "Gracie. All you have to do is walk. Walk down the dirt road until you come to a paved road. Okay?"

"But I don't want to go out there alone."

"Ten…" Cassidy leaned a shoulder against the door-jamb and folded her arms. "Nine…"

"Hey." Shae wiped the tears from Gracie's cheeks and fought back her own. "You won't be alone, baby. God is always with you. Just pray as you walk and try to stay calm, okay?"

"Eight…"

Her little girl sucked in a deep, shaky breath. "Okay, Mommy."

"Seven…"

"Go, baby. Go now."

"Six…five…"

"I love you, baby girl, with all my heart."

"Four…"

"I love you, too, Mommy."

"Three…two…"

Gracie walked out the door. She looked back at Shae over her shoulder once, then lifted her chin and strode down the steps and started across the clearing.

Cassidy shut the door behind her. "She's a strong kid. I give her a fifty percent chance of making it. Either way, we'll be long gone before she can reach civilization and lead anyone back here."

Shae lunged and landed a solid punch to Cassidy's jaw.

Cassidy shoved her off and pointed the weapon at her.

"Don't forget, my men can easily catch up with her. And if you try anything like that again, they will."

Shae clenched her fists at her sides, sucked in deep lungfuls of stale, musty air. "Why are you doing this? I don't understand."

Cassidy's mouth firmed into a tight line, her grip on the weapon tightening. "Four years ago, my husband and son were killed."

Pain stabbed Shae's heart. "I'm sorry."

"Sorry? Sorry?" She shoved Shae back with the weapon. "You know what sorry does to bring my family back? Nothing!"

"Cassidy, please. If you know what it's like to lose a child, how could—"

The slap came fast and hard, a backhand that left the coppery taste of blood filling her mouth. "Don't you dare use my grief to try to worm your way out of this."

"I didn't mean it that way, I just—"

"Do you know what happened when the FBI, the agency I devoted my life to, found their killer?"

Shae shook her head.

"They offered him immunity to testify against Antonio Pesci. The guy was one of his higher-level lieutenants, and he killed my family because I was on the team that went after Pesci for assault, money laundering and attempted murder. Of course, our witness was killed, leaving us with nothing, because the lieutenant they'd traded away my family's justice for was found dead in prison." She shoved a single tear away with the heel of her hand, and her expression hardened. Whatever bit of emotion had surfaced at the thought of the tragedy that had befallen her family disappeared in an instant, to be replaced by bitterness and anger Shae could at least understand, if not condone. "I guess bringing Pesci down was worth more than the lives of my husband and child, and they couldn't even manage to get it right."

"So, how did you get involved with Sebastian Kincaid?" Shae tried to keep her tone even, keep her talking. While her heart ached for this woman's loss, it didn't excuse her decision to work with the Kincaids and betray everyone she knew.

"Sebastian?" She laughed, a horrible, evil sound. "Honey, I have no involvement with Sebastian. As a matter of fact, by the time I finish with you and walk out of here, Sebastian will have followed his father into the grave."

Shae shook her head, trying to clear the confusion, trying to see past thoughts of Gracie wandering alone through the Florida forest so she could think. She hadn't planned anything past getting Cassidy to drop Gracie off somewhere safe. Now that she'd tossed her daughter out on her own, Shae had to try to get to her. And the only way to do that would be to go through Cassidy Monroe. She wasn't sure how yet, so she had to stall, to give herself time to come up with a plan to get past not only Cassidy, but the armed gunmen she'd stationed outside.

"Regina," Shae said, realization dawning.

"Regina," Cassidy agreed.

"But I thought she had nothing to do with the Kincaid organization."

"Of course she does. But she's smarter than her brother. She went to college, learned all she'd need to know in order to run the Kincaid empire while her brother hung around trying to follow in his daddy's footsteps like some kind of trained dog. While Sebastian racked up a criminal record, Regina got a degree. While Sebastian spent his life taking orders, Regina learned how to lead. And now that the time has come, she's making her play for the top spot."

"That's why Regina didn't move on me when she first found me. She was waiting for Quentin to die, then she was going to kill me and take over the family business instead of her brother."

"Almost. She was waiting for Quentin to be *near* death. That was the deal they made—he always promised he'd give her a chance to take over. He believed in her brains, saw more potential in her than he did Sebastian. Apparently, it's even spelled out in a document containing his final wishes and held onto by his lawyer. He'd name a target before he died, and whoever got the target won the empire. A risky power play, but a necessary one. A way to prove she commands resources Sebastian couldn't hope to wield."

For a moment, Shae remembered the man she'd worked for who'd always encouraged and praised Shae's own intelligence and creativity. She banished it from her mind. "But Sebastian was part of the organization for years. He must have contacts, loyalty—"

Cassidy spat on the floor. "Sebastian has nothing. He *is* nothing. Regina put her own lieutenant in place to undermine him every step of the way. And now she'll take over the Kincaid organization and it will become the most powerful family in the country."

Shae frowned. Something wasn't adding up. "So why am I still alive? And why did you take Gracie from the safe house when you could have grabbed me at any time?"

"We wanted you alive, needed you alive. We couldn't risk a shootout, knowing you'd sacrifice your life to save your daughter if it came down to it. It was better for me to wait, bide my time until I could slip away with Gracie. I figured she'd be easier to handle and then we could use her to lure you out, but the brat started screaming the minute she heard her stupid dog barking. I tried to get her out, but I ended up having to kill everyone."

Keep her talking, keep her talking. "That's why you took Gracie. Okay. But why do you need me alive? You already know who was protecting me, which apparently no one shared with Sebastian, so what is it you want from me?"

"The project you came across when you were working for Quentin Kincaid."

"Project?" What was she talking about? "You mean the attack he had planned on the Pesci family?"

"Exactly."

"What about it?"

"You're going to recreate it." She lifted her chin in defiance. "Regina is going to finish what her father started. And I am going to get justice, revenge, whatever, for my family. I'm going to get even with Antonio Pesci—wipe out his entire family just like he did mine."

"No." No way would Shae be complicit in a plan that would kill anyone, even a crime family. Besides, who knew how many innocent lives might be endangered in the process?

"I was afraid you'd say that." She whipped open the front door. "Go get the girl."

"No. Wait. Please." Shae had spent several terrifying weeks gathering information after she'd overheard that first awful conversation. She knew the blueprints well, the ones for the building where the Pescis' infamous New Year's Eve party always took place. The breath rushed from her lungs as she finally understood. It was the one time of year the whole family and all the highest-ranking associates gathered, and the place had better security than a prison. Regina needed the details Shae had memorized before going to the police. "New Year's Eve."

"That's right. You might have had more time with your daughter if Quentin was in better health. But since he named you as the target—just like Regina knew he would—so close to New Year's, Regina sees it as fortuitous timing. Help me now, and we don't go after the girl. And maybe you'll live to see your daughter again."

Shae only nodded. No way would she put Gracie's life in danger, but she couldn't give them the plans to kill the Pesci family, either.

"I thought you might change your mind."

Mason crept silently through the thick undergrowth parallel to the dirt road. It was perfect cover as he moved toward the cabin Zac's team had tracked Shae to. He ignored the chatter over the comms as Zac placed his agents around the perimeter and coordinated the rescue attempt. Mason had only one objective: get to Shae and Gracie, and he would see to that with single-minded determination.

The crunch of dried brush to his right had him pausing. He crouched low and turned toward the sound. Nothing. He started to turn away.

"Please, help me find help." A whisper reached through the silence, and a little voice said, "And please, save Mommy," followed by soft sobs.

His heart shattered into a million pieces as he changed direction to intercept his daughter. He found her walking on the side of the dirt road, praying through her tears. Though he hated the thought of scaring her, he couldn't take a chance she'd scream and draw attention. He waited for her to pass his position, then slid out behind her. In one smooth motion, he scooped her up and hugged her against his chest with one hand and covered her mouth with the other, then whispered urgently, "It's okay, Gracie. It's me. It's…" *Daddy…* "Mason."

Her body went limp in his arms, and she turned to face him, then wrapped her arms around his neck and hugged him.

Mason held on tight, buried his face against her shoulder and inhaled deeply the scents of baby shampoo and sweat. "It's okay, Gracie. You're okay now."

She cried so hard her entire body shook. "I want my mommy."

"I know, honey." He could have stood there forever, the weight of his daughter in his arms, the assurance she was safe, the pure love he felt for the first time in six years flowing through him unfettered. But he had to get to Shae.

With one look around to be sure he hadn't been seen, he ducked back into the woods. "Are you hurt?"

She shook her head against him, her tears soaking his neck. "Cassidy took me, and she had a gun, and she wouldn't let Mommy go."

"I know, honey. I know. I'm going to go get her.

Okay?" He lowered Gracie to her feet and knelt in front of her, shifted her back so he could look her in the eye, eyes that matched his own, right down to the terror he saw reflected there. "Listen to me, Gracie, okay?"

She nodded, sniffed, her eyes so swollen from crying they were practically slits.

"I'm going to get your mommy, but I have to make sure you're safe before I can do that." He tapped the button on his communicator to summon help, then pulled Gracie into his lap and held her close. "I am so proud of you, Gracie. I know you're scared. I'm scared, too, but together we're going to get through this. I promise. I'm going to go get your mommy and bring her back to you, and then…"

And then what? He loved Shae absolutely, fiercely, with everything in him. He'd never stopped loving her, even if he'd been too stubborn to accept it, but was there a future for them? A nice little family with a small house in the suburbs, a golden retriever and a white picket fence? Even if they could get Shae and Gracie relocated somewhere they'd be safe, what then? The work Mason did…that was no life for Shae. To have her husband pop in every now and then, emotionally damaged from whatever atrocities he'd witnessed and had to turn a blind eye to in order to maintain his cover? And what about Gracie? What kind of unstable life was that for a child who'd been through so much trauma already? At one time, he'd been willing to give up his career to go into witness protection with Shae. But things had changed. He'd made it his mission to help those the Kincaids went after.

He was saved from having to search for answers when Angela emerged from the woods. Cradling Gracie in his arms, he stood, kissed her tangled hair. "Gracie, honey, I need you stay with Angela so I can go get Mommy. Okay?"

She eyed Angela with suspicion.

"You can trust her, Gracie. She's the one person I know will keep you safe." Tremors coursed through him as he handed Gracie into Angela's arms. "Please, Angela. Stay with her. Don't leave her with anyone else."

"You have my word, Mason." She hugged Gracie against her and rubbed a hand up and down her back. "I'll care for her like she's my own."

"Look who I found, Gracie." Mason reached into his pack, pulled out Mr. Cuddles and pressed him gently into Gracie's arms.

"You found him!" She hugged the stuffed bunny tight, her sobs reducing to sniffles. "Cassidy let me take him. But I dropped him on the grass when she put me in the car so Mommy would know."

"Oh, Gracie." Love poured through him. He kissed her head. "You are so smart and so brave. You're amazing, Gracie."

"Mommy says we have to stay calm and think in an emergency."

"Well, you certainly did. Your mommy is going to be so proud of you. I'm so proud of you."

She laid her head against him, her arms still wrapped around Angela's neck. Then she straightened up. "Can you go find Mommy now?"

"Yes, honey. I'm going right now." Turning away from her in that moment was one of the most difficult things he'd ever done. But Shae needed him, and he would not fail her. He resumed his trek through the woods, listening intently to catch up on where Zac's men were positioned. When he reached the clearing, he slid behind a tree and trained his binoculars on the woods surrounding the cabin. He leashed every ounce of control he possessed to keep from charging across the clearing and into that cabin. It was time to get his head in the game. "How many hostiles?"

"Six outside, one in." Zac's hushed voice in his ear brought reassurance. "Four around the perimeter, two on the front porch. Heat signatures inside show two people, one on their knees, one standing, both by the front door."

Urgency begged him not to wait any longer. "We have to move."

"Our people are about to intercept the four guarding the woods."

"Which leaves taking out the two on the porch—quietly."

"One for me, and one for you."

Mason stayed in the woods as he rounded the cabin, positioning himself slightly behind so he wouldn't be seen approaching, and waited for the signal that the four combatants in the woods had been removed. Zac's people were good. Even from Mason's position nearby, he didn't see or hear any sign of trouble. But now they had to move fast, before anyone looked for the missing guards.

Crossing the clearing would be the most dangerous part. If they were seen, he had no doubt Cassidy would kill Shae instantly. He shoved the thought aside—couldn't let it interfere.

"It's a go," Zac said.

Mason emerged from the woods and ran in a low

crouch across the clearing, then placed his back against the rear wall of the cabin and took a breath. A quick glance showed Zac leaning against the wall at the far side. He signaled to Mason, and they each slipped around opposite sides of the cabin. Mason crept forward, mindful of every step, every breath, moving as silently as any other predator roaming these woods.

When he reached the edge of the porch, he used a small mirror around the corner to check the positions of the guards. They stood on either end of the porch that ran the full width of the cabin, each cradling an automatic weapon. It was imperative he and Zac move together. They'd coordinated attacks before and could move almost as one.

"Go." Barely a whisper of sound, but all Mason needed.

He rounded the corner, vaulted the railing. The gunman must have sensed a presence, because he turned. His eyes went wide as he lifted the weapon. Mason took his shot, muffled by the silencer, then caught the guy and eased him soundlessly to the porch.

He stayed low, ducking beneath the window, held his breath. Listened. Nothing. He crept to the door while Zac attached an electronic surveillance device to the window and patched the sound through to Mason. An agent in a van at the end of the road would monitor and record the transmission for later evaluation, but in the meantime, it might provide Zac and Mason with an opening to enter and apprehend Cassidy without any further loss of life. Unfortunately, they'd had no choice but to kill the two guards on the porch, but the four in the woods had simply been rendered unconscious and would live to testify and pay for their crimes.

Shae's voice came through his earpiece, shaky but strong. "…the layout as best I can remember, but I don't recall how many devices were set or exactly where they were positioned."

Zac frowned at him.

Mason shrugged and shook his head once. He had no idea what they were talking about, but it didn't matter as long as Shae was all right. He studied the door—just one dead-bolt lock, as far as he could tell. Blinds across the front windows were closed, so he couldn't see in. But Cassidy couldn't see out, either, so he considered that a plus. Either way, they had to assume Cassidy had a weapon. But did she have it aimed at Shae?

He breathed in deeply and let it out, smooth and slow…waiting…waiting… Energy vibrated through him.

The image of Shae kneeling before Cassidy, terrified that her daughter was roaming the woods alone, in fear for her life, seared itself into his brain. "Victim is still kneeling. Suspect standing in front of her, arms at her sides."

Okay, good. That gave them the extra split second she would need to lift a weapon and aim it at Shae. A fraction of a second that would determine the rest of Shae's life, Gracie's life. His life. He didn't know how he and Shae were going to make things work between them, but he knew with every ounce of his being that he was going to try. The thought of losing her, of watching her die while he was helpless to stop it, was more than he could bear.

Okay, he could do this. As long as he put thoughts

of Shae out of his mind. He'd done this many times as an FBI agent without so much as a hitch in his breathing or a spike in his heart rate. And this time, he was going through the door with Zac, his friend, a man he trusted with his life. Sweat slicked his hands, beaded at his temples.

Zac gestured two agents to move in with a battering ram.

This was it. He sucked in a breath, held it. *One... two...three—*

The door crashed open beneath the force of the ram.

Mason dived in, going low while Zac went high, and then he was in front of Shae, staring down Cassidy Monroe, his weapon held steady as he stood between Shae and danger. "Drop the weapon, Cassidy."

She froze, weapon half raised as if trying to decide if it was worth trying to escape. Her eyes flicked from side to side, taking in where Zac stood, weapon trained on her, then back to Mason.

"Don't do it, Cassidy." While anger surged through him at this woman who'd befriended Shae, her daughter, the agents she'd killed at the house—all of whom she'd betrayed—he didn't want to have to fire a fatal shot. "Lower the weapon. You can't escape. You know that, Cassidy."

He could feel Shae's presence behind him, sense her fear, but she remained perfectly still, absolutely silent.

"Drop it, Cassidy. Two of your men are already dead, and the other four are in custody. There's nowhere to go, no one to intervene. The cabin is surrounded." He had to get through to her, had to get her to give up without a fight. Had to find out what they'd been talking about.

What devices? Did it have anything to do with the C-4 they'd confiscated? He lifted his weapon, firmed his stance. "Now, Cassidy. Drop it."

She must have sensed something in him, because she straightened, removed her finger from the trigger and raised her hands.

Zac moved in, cuffed her and hustled her outside.

The instant Zac had secured the suspect and no threat remained, Mason turned to Shae and held out a hand. "Are you okay?"

She grabbed his hand, surged to her feet and started toward the door. "Gracie!"

"It's okay, she's safe." He hooked her arm, turned her to face him and smoothed her hair back out of her face, cradling her cheeks between his hands. "She's safe, Shae. We have her. I found her walking down the road. She's with Angela now. Only Angela. She'll protect our daughter with her life. I promise."

"She's okay?" Tears spilled over her lashes, streamed with a mix of eye makeup down red, blotchy cheeks. And she'd never looked more beautiful. He closed his eyes, savoring the moment, pressed his forehead against hers. "She's not only fine, but an amazing, courageous, beautiful little girl."

"Mason?" Zac stood in the doorway. "I'm sorry to interrupt, but Cassidy's talking."

ELEVEN

Shae sat in the back of the surveillance van, listening to Zac's instructions for the third time while Mason seethed nearby. She knew he didn't want her to do this. So did everyone else in attendance, since he'd voiced his opinion quite…energetically.

"Just speak normally." Zac fiddled with some adjustment or another to make sure everything Regina Kincaid said was caught and recorded.

"Testing. One, two, three." She was going to do this. She had no choice. Well, that wasn't true. She *could* spend the rest of her life in hiding, praying every day that Gracie wouldn't be targeted again. Or she could put an end to this once and for all by confronting Regina Kincaid while wearing a wire. If she could get Regina to incriminate herself Zac's team could take her into custody. For now, they were working together with local law enforcement, but Zac had decided to leave the FBI out of the operation until they could figure out who else might be compromised and clean house.

Zac looked her in the eye, his scrutiny intense. "Are you sure, Shae?"

"Positive. I can do this." She hoped her voice held

more conviction than she actually felt. Though she was determined to make this work, she wasn't all that confident in her ability to do so. She just hoped he didn't notice how badly she was shaking and terminate the operation.

He nodded and stepped back. "Okay. I'll be right back, and we'll get started."

Once Zac emerged from the van, leaving Shae and Mason alone, she turned to him. "I'm sorry, Mason. I know you don't think I'm doing the right thing, but I have to do this. I have to end this. Please try to understand."

"Ah, man, Shae." He sat on the bench across from her, gripped her hands in his. "It's not that I don't agree with you. In my head I know this is the right call, the only way to assure your and Gracie's safety. And if it was anyone else, I'd be all for it. It's my heart that's having a tough time. I just wish it wasn't you who had to go in. You know if I could, I would."

She squeezed his hands, pressed her lips against his knuckles. "I know, but I'm the only one who might be able to get a recorded confession. Cassidy's testimony might not be enough." If what Cassidy had shared was true, at least they didn't have to worry about Sebastian any longer. Apparently, Regina had had her brother killed, his body dumped in a lake, where police divers were currently searching for his remains.

"I know." He blew out a breath. "I know. But that doesn't mean I have to like it."

A smile tugged at her. She wanted so badly for this nightmare to end. She and Mason hadn't had time to talk after Cassidy gave up Regina's location, but she knew they needed to. One way or the other, they had to come to some kind of resolution, especially if he wanted to be a part of Gracie's life. *Gracie.* She lowered her gaze to their clasped hands.

The decision not to go to Gracie immediately after Mason had rescued her from the cabin had been heart-wrenching. But it wouldn't have been fair. Though Mason, Zac and his agents would make this operation run as smoothly and safely as possible, there was still an element of danger involved. There was always the chance Regina would kill her on sight, which was, hopefully, minimized by the fact that Shae had information the wannabe crime boss needed. And there was a risk she'd discover the wire, in which case she'd kill Shae, but at least she'd be taken into custody immediately after and charged with murder, so Gracie would be safe. Either way, Shae didn't think it was fair to go to Gracie, make her think that things were over and Shae would stay with her, and then turn around and walk back out again.

She leaned her head back against the side of the van. Plus, if Gracie had begged her not to go, what would she have done? She wouldn't have been able to say no, would have stayed despite the lives her decision might cost…

Her thoughts stuttered to a stop. Weren't those the exact same reasons Mason had given for why he'd left without saying goodbye six years ago? *Ah, man…* "Mason?"

"Yeah."

"I'm so sorry."

"Sorry?" He frowned. "For what?"

"I forgave you long ago for leaving me, but until this moment, I didn't fully understand how you could have done so. And now I do."

"Shae…"

"It's okay. I don't know where things will go from here if we make it through the next few hours, but I know I want you to be a part of our lives. In whatever capacity you're able to make work. If that's what you want…"

As he opened his mouth, the door swung open. Zac stood in the doorway. "It's time, Shae."

She inhaled deeply, blew it out slowly and stood. "I'm ready."

Mason massaged her shoulders. "You remember what to do and say?"

"Yes." It wasn't like this was the first time she'd worn a wire. But still, the reminder comforted her.

"Speak clearly but not too loud, or it will alert her that you're wearing a wire." He handed her the weapon Cassidy had been holding at the cabin. "The microphone is sensitive enough to easily pick up your voice."

"Got it." She tucked the weapon into her waistband. Thankfully, Mason didn't try to stop her as she stalked across the parking lot toward the motel room Cassidy had indicated. If he had, there was a good chance she'd have backed out.

When she reached the door, she barely resisted the urge to look over her shoulder and assure herself Mason and the other agents were in place. But Mason and Zac had both drilled it into her head. *Walk straight across the lot, determined but wary. Do not look over your shoulder and give the operation away.*

She lifted a hand, fisted it and knocked on the door. "Who is it?"

"Shae…uh, I mean, Avery Bennett." Funny, she'd only been Shae Evans for six years, yet that was the name that felt more comfortable. Was that what it was like for Mason when going undercover? "I need to talk to you. Now."

Silence. Well, at least she hadn't shot her though the door.

"Cassidy and her men are…" She looked around then as if making sure no one would overhear her, in case Regina was looking through the peephole. She injected a pleading note into her tone, letting her desperation show. "Out of the picture. I just want to talk. Please."

Regina cracked the door open, surveyed the area, then stepped back and gestured Shae in with her pistol and slammed the door behind her. "What are you talking about, out of the picture?"

"I…lost my cool when they tossed my five-year-old daughter out of the cabin in the middle of the woods by herself." She allowed her voice to rise, allowed her rage to show. It was no act. "I was willing to give you what you wanted to keep my child safe, but that witch not only betrayed me, but she didn't even give Gracie a chance. All I asked was that she drop her off somewhere safe, and I would have given you anything."

Shae sucked in a few deep breaths, struggled to contain her anger. She massaged the bridge of her nose between a thumb and forefinger, then lifted her hands in the air. "Okay. Full disclosure. I have Cassidy's weapon in my waistband. I'm not gonna lie, I thought about just coming here and shooting you after Cassidy told me where to find you—"

"There's no way Cassidy ratted me out." Regina took the weapon from Shae, placed it on a nearby table, then patted her down for more weapons and came up empty.

Thankfully, she didn't notice the tiny recording device disguised as a button on her blouse.

"Yeah, well, she was mighty chatty when she thought I was going to be dead shortly. How else would I have known you'd be alone here, not surrounded by protection because you don't even trust your own people?" Shae shrugged as if it didn't matter. "Either way, all I care about is Gracie. I want my daughter safe. I don't want to spend the rest of my life looking over my shoulder, wondering where the next attack will come from."

The younger woman tilted her head, studied Shae. "So why not just kill me?"

"Because then I have to worry about retaliation from your brother."

Regina simply nodded.

When Shae's chin started to tremble, she didn't bother to firm it. She let the tears leak from her eyes, showed how vulnerable she was. "Please, Regina. All I want to do is get my daughter and go back home. I want to live in peace with her. Please. I'll do whatever it takes to make that happen."

She tilted her head, narrowed her eyes. "Even if that means helping me take out the Pescis?"

Nausea turned Shae's stomach, even though she knew that wasn't going to happen. "Sure. That's on you, not me."

"And what's to keep you from going to the police?"

"The police can't protect us. You think I haven't learned that lesson yet?"

A slow smile spread. "That's right, and don't you forget that. My reach is far and wide."

Shae nodded and lowered her head, no longer vulnerable but defeated.

"I'll accept your terms. You give me the information I want, and I give you my word you and your daughter will remain safe." Regina grinned, her eyes lighting with pure evil. "As long as my New Year's Eve plan goes off without any interference from the law."

"Fair enough. And you'll be able to keep Sebastian from coming after me as well?" If she could get her to admit to his murder, this would end right now.

"Sebastian won't be a problem."

It had been a long shot, hoping she'd boast that she'd ordered her brother's murder, but Shae was still disappointed when she didn't elaborate. "Can you pull up a blueprint of the target, or do I need to draw it out?"

"You'll draw out the diagram, mark where each of the devices should be placed for maximum carnage. If I believe you're telling me the truth, I'll pull up a blueprint and you'll show me the access points into the building and the security we need to evade."

Shae pulled out a chair and sat at the small round table. "I'll need a pen and paper."

Still keeping the weapon aimed at Shae, the younger woman dug through a briefcase and came up with a legal pad and pen, then sat across from her, weapon resting on the table, and slid them across to her.

"Can I ask you something?" Shae lifted the pen, her hand shaking so badly she was afraid she might drop it, and started to sketch an outline of the building where the Pescis hosted their annual New Year's Eve party. "Why are you doing this? Why bother killing the Pescis when you will soon have control of the more powerful family anyway?"

She laughed out loud, tossed her hair. "I'm going to kill

the Pescis because they're a threat. I've neutralized every threat I've ever faced—and that includes Sebastian."

Shae didn't hesitate when the door banged open. She simply tipped her chair and let herself fall, landing hard on her shoulder.

"Police! Freeze!"

Regina lunged to her feet, lifted her weapon toward Shae. "You—"

Mason's shot took her in the shoulder, and her weapon clattered to the floor.

A beehive of activity carried on around her, but Shae paid attention to none of it, her full focus on Mason as he helped her up.

"Are you hurt?"

"No. I'm okay." Though her shoulder would no doubt ache tomorrow, along with her chest and, well, pretty much everything.

"Shae." A small chuckle emerged, and Mason shook his head. "This is so not the time for this, and yet, somehow strangely appropriate."

She frowned, unsure what he was talking about.

He cradled her face between his hands in a gesture that had always brought comfort and that soothed now.

She tilted her cheek into his hand, let his warmth seep through her.

"I love you, Shae. With everything in me, with all my heart, and I don't want to live another minute without you." He eased her close, pressed his lips to hers, then leaned back just enough to look into her eyes. "I love you, and I love Gracie. I don't know the logistics of it all yet..."

Leave it to Mason to make starting a life together sound like a carefully planned field operation.

"But I know I want the three of us to be together."

Joy filled her, and she threw her arms around his neck. "Oh, Mason. I love you, too. I never stopped."

"She's here, Mason," Zac called from the doorway.

He wrapped an arm around Shae's shoulders, kissed her temple. "Come on. Gracie's waiting."

"She's here? You brought her here?" They were going to have to set some ground rules. One—don't take Gracie to crime scenes. But she laughed, unbelievably happy. Not only was this years-long ordeal finally over, and Gracie and Shae both finally out of danger, but Mason was back in her life—their lives—as well. A better outcome than she ever could have dreamed of.

Together, they crossed the parking lot to the diner across the street. When they rounded the back of the building, she spotted Gracie anxiously shifting back and forth beside Angela.

The instant she spotted Shae, she screamed, "Mommy," barreled across the lot and launched herself into Shae's arms.

"Oh, baby." Shae hugged Gracie tight. She might never let go. "I love you, baby. I love you so much."

Mason wrapped them both in his embrace.

Gracie lifted her head and looked back and forth between Shae and Mason. "Can we go home now?"

The realization they could return to the life they'd built in Boggy Meadows hit her. "Yes, baby. Come on. Let's go home."

EPILOGUE

Mason hefted the wiggling ball of golden fur into his arms and slammed the car door shut. Though he and Shae had talked about getting Gracie a puppy after Storm had gone back to his handler, the past year had been filled with one thing after another, both good and bad. They'd yet to talk much past the initial idea.

He scratched the puppy's head. "You be a good boy, now, ya hear? Don't go getting me in trouble."

The puppy wagged his whole back end, hopefully in agreement or possibly just itching to escape Mason's grasp and find some kind of trouble.

He shifted his bundle under his arm so he could dig out his key. Sometimes he still couldn't believe Shae and Gracie were a permanent part of his life. Even now, four months after he and Shae had gotten married in a small ceremony with Gracie between them, and Zac, Angela, Reva and Katie in attendance, there were plenty of nights he still woke terrified they'd be taken from him. But, over time, the nightmares would lessen. He hoped.

"Here we go, boy." He sucked in a deep breath, braced himself and pushed the front door open. "Shae? Gracie?"

Silence greeted him.

He forced back the momentary panic, tamped down the surge of terror and reminded himself there was no longer any reason to fear for their safety. As of today. He tossed his keys on the tray in the foyer. "I'm home, guys. Anyone here?"

Gracie's laughter skittered down the hallway, and he followed the sound through the small house to the backyard. They'd settled back in Boggy Meadows, with Mason working for Jameson Investigations behind the scenes rather than in the field, but they'd sold the house where Shae and Gracie had been attacked. They'd bought a new one together, a four-bedroom ranch with an office where Shae could still work from home and a big yard for Gracie to run around in.

He slid the back door open, then leaned a shoulder against the doorjamb and petted the puppy's head as he watched Gracie squeal while Shae pushed her on a swing.

The instant Gracie spotted him, she let go of the chains and swung off, landing perfectly and giving Mason a small heart attack. "Mommy, Daddy's home!"

Even after a year to get used to it, those words still had the power to drive him to his knees. He'd found his faith again, and he thanked God every night for bringing Shae and Gracie into his life.

"And he brought a puppy!" She bolted across the lawn and held her arms open. "Can I hold him?"

"Sure thing, baby girl." He handed the puppy over.

"Whose is he?" She nuzzled him against her cheek.

He glanced at Shae, who'd come up behind Gracie and stood with a huge smile on her face. He put his arm around her shoulders, pulled her close so he could kiss her temple, then whispered, "It's done."

Shae went still, and he simply smiled, then said to their daughter, "He's yours, Gracie."

"Ahh!" She set the puppy down, then flung her arms around his and Shae's legs. "Thank you, thank you, thank you."

He couldn't help but laugh. "You're welcome, honey."

And then she was off, running laps with the puppy around the fenced yard. "We talked about getting a puppy but never fully decided when…"

"He's perfect, Mason." She wrapped both arms around his waist. "Is it really over?"

"Yes. Regina was convicted today. They got her on first-degree murder in Sebastian's death and conspiracy to commit murder for the Pesci plan." Cassidy was already serving time in federal prison, a reduced but heavy sentence in exchange for her testimony against Regina.

Shae leaned into him, and he took the moment to savor having her close, watching Gracie and the puppy run and play together. Then she looked up. "I think I took the addition of the puppy very well, don't you?"

"Yes." He frowned. Not sure where she was going with this, since she'd technically already agreed to the puppy, if not the timing.

"Well, now it's your turn." A smile played at the corner of her mouth.

"What do you mean?"

"Seems a puppy won't be the only addition to our family today."

"Wha…" Everything in him went still. "Are you saying what I think you're saying?"

"Yes, Mason. You're going to be a dad again."

Emotions poured through him, and love swamped him, threatened to drown him. He pulled Shae into his arms, lifted her off the ground and swung her around, then thought better of it and lowered her gently. "I'm sorry. Was that okay?"

Her laughter filled him with joy as she flipped her long hair behind her shoulder and looked up at him from beneath her lashes. "It was fine. I'm not that fragile."

"No, you're not fragile at all. In fact, you're one of the strongest women I know. It's one of the things I love most about you. But, that said…" He guided her toward a lounge chair. "You should sit and rest."

"I don't need to rest."

He sat on the edge of the chair beside her leg and clutched her hand. "What do you need? Because I'm going to be here this time, Shae, and I am going to take care of you, and spoil you, and—"

"I don't need to be spoiled, I just need you to love me."

"I do, Shae. I love you, and Gracie, and our new baby…" The thought brought so much joy he was practically light-headed. "With every last bit of my heart."

* * * * *

   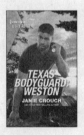